THE STOLEN CHILD

EMILY SHINER

INKUBATOR
BOOKS

Published by Inkubator Books
www.inkubatorbooks.com

ISBN (eBook): 978-1-83756-000-4
ISBN (Paperback): 978-1-83756-001-1
ISBN (Hardback): 978-1-83756-002-8

PROLOGUE
ELIZA

"Are you sure this is the house?" My husband, James, sounds more disgusted than confused, like he honestly can't believe I'm going to set foot in the house in front of us. We're on the porch, both of us carefully balancing our weight so that we don't break through the rotten planks of wood.

"This is it." I check the scrap of paper I have in my pocket, even though I already know that this is the right place. "It's the last place she was living, anyway."

He makes a noncommittal sound deep in his throat, and I push past him to knock on the door. At the first touch of my knuckles, it swings in, the hinges crying out as it does. A wave of thick air washes over the two of us, and I reach up, covering my mouth.

James sucks in a breath. "Is that...?"

"Smells like the plumbing is out." I don't turn back to him to see the expression on his face as I step inside. "Hello? Camilla?" My sister's name feels foreign in my mouth. "Camilla, are you here?"

There's no answer. I reach over, trying to flick on the light switch. My fingers drag through something wet on the wall, and I recoil, then pull my phone from my pocket to use the flashlight instead.

"No power?" James murmurs. "How in the world is she living here without power and plumbing?"

"She probably shouldn't be." I snap the words at him as I shine my phone's flashlight around the living room. There's a sagging sofa in the corner covered with stains and an old coffee table in front of it. Even though I've never done drugs, I see needles and spoons on the table in between empty beer cans, and I shine the flashlight in the other direction.

It's one thing to know that your sister is throwing away her life on drugs, and another to see it all played out right before your eyes.

A soft thunk from the hall gets our attention; I'm glad to look away from the stack of moldy boxes in the other side of the room. I'm half-tempted to look through them, to try to tell what Camilla might find so important she wants to keep it even though the rest of her life is falling apart, but the thunk comes again, and James brushes past me, bumping my elbow so the light zigzags across the dark room.

"Where are you going?" I hiss, suddenly scared to take another step into my sister's house. "You don't know who might be back there."

Real fear prickles the back of my neck, and I feel my hair stand straight up. Maybe this is stupid. Maybe we should have called the police to come with us, but I can only imagine how they would treat Camilla once they saw her. Cops don't like druggies, don't like people who can't pay their bills, don't generally care to be kind to the people society has cast aside.

But still, what if we meet Camilla's dealer? What if she got her hands on a gun; what if she decides she really doesn't want us here?

Fear grips my throat, and I have to force myself to follow

James down the hall. By now, he has his phone out, the light steady in his hand as he walks towards the back of the house. I glance in a bathroom, the source of the terrible smell, then follow James through the single door at the end of the hall.

It's her bedroom.

There's not a bed, because of course she wouldn't have kept anything she could sell for drug money. Instead of a bed, there's a single mattress on the floor, covered with stains from God-knows-what. My sister is passed out on her back, her arm slung out to the side, her mouth open at a funny angle.

"Is she alive?" Even though it should be obvious to me that Camilla isn't the one who made the thunk we heard earlier, all I can think about is my sister. I drop to my knees next to her, reaching out and holding my hand above her mouth.

It takes a moment, but I feel it.

Soft breaths. Barely there, more like the memory of wind than anything else, but she's breathing.

"Eliza." James sounds stressed.

I get it; I do. This is the last place he wanted to come today, and I practically had to beg him to get out of the car and come with me. It took promising that we could leave Penelope with his college friends, and that we wouldn't be gone longer than it took to make sure Camilla was alive, to get him to come here with me.

I haven't seen her in years, haven't even heard from her. It was guilt over the thought of what my estranged sister might be doing that led me to find her here in Canada, to hunt her down. Thank goodness James has friends close by that we could stop in and visit, so the trip here wouldn't be just about finding her.

There really wasn't any way of knowing what we would find in here.

So of course he's stressed.

"Just a minute," I say, holding one finger in the air as I reach out with my other hand to brush Camilla's hair off her cheek. It looks like I should be able to tuck it behind her ear, but it's stuck to her skin with sweat or vomit or beer, and I jerk my hand back.

"Eliza." The stress in James' voice is still there, but it's undercut by something else.

"Hang on." I try again, suddenly unwilling to leave Camilla here with her hair stuck to her cheek. She's my little sister and has always been a screwup, but I promised myself I'd do my best to take care of her when we both aged out of foster care. I told myself I'd try my best to keep her safe and stop her from spiraling more than she had.

This is my last-ditch attempt to do just that.

"Eliza!"

"What?" Whipping around, I shine my cell phone's flashlight up at James. His face is drawn, tight. "What is it?"

He doesn't answer. I finally drag my eyes away from his face, away from the light cast on his pale skin, to where he's shining his light.

It's shining on a little boy dressed in a sagging diaper, his thumb in his mouth, his eyes wide with fear. He has blond hair matted down to his head, and there's a stuffed animal clutched to his chest.

At least, I think it's a stuffed animal. It's stained and probably smelly, but the little boy, who's staring at me like I'm a ghost, doesn't look like he's about to let it go.

"Does your sister have a kid?" James sounds like he's choking.

I shake my head, standing and moving slowly over to the little boy.

He's what we heard thunking as we came down the hall.

As I get closer to him, I can not only see how his ribs stick out a little bit, but I can smell him. He's rank, his diaper needing to be changed hours and hours ago. My heart breaks.

"She never told me she had a kid," I say, squatting down in front of the boy. "How old are you?"

He doesn't answer. Instead, he sucks his thumb harder, pressing his stuffed animal into his chest. This close to him I can see that it's a rabbit, or was, and he has it gripped by the ears.

"What's your name?" I try again, my heart beating wildly in my chest. "Is Camilla your mommy?"

Nothing.

"We have to call the cops." The light shining on the boy disappears as James starts to tap on his phone. "They need to come deal with this."

"No." My answer surprises both of us as I stand up and grab James by the wrist. His finger is right above the green call button, and I squeeze hard to get his attention. "No, don't call the cops. They won't help."

"Won't help?" He sputters the words at me. "Eliza, what do you think we have police for? They can help by taking this little boy. Camilla can go into a facility."

"She won't and you know it." Slowly, like I need to make sure he's not going to make a call, I let go of his arm, then chew my fingernail before I remember how disgusting this house is and drop my hand to my side. "James, we can't make this little boy go into foster care."

I won't do it. I won't be the reason another kid has to go through the same hell I did when I was younger.

"Well, we certainly can't leave him." My husband crosses his arms. "Do you have a better idea? Because our daughter is waiting for us to pick her up, and then we have a long drive home. Whatever we do, we need to do it quickly so that this doesn't become a huge deal."

I turn and look at my sister, unable to voice the thought

eating at the back of my mind. The two of us aren't being quiet while we talk, but she still hasn't moved. "She might die," I say.

"She might."

"And then where would this little boy be?" I look down at him again, fighting the urge to reach out and ruffle his hair. He's filthy and needs a bath, some clean clothes, and a good meal. "It looks like she wakes up just enough to take care of him from time to time, but someone has to be there for him all the time."

There's a beat of silence before James understands what I'm saying. "No, Eliza. Not a chance. We're not taking him."

I turn to him, ripping my eyes from the little boy. From my nephew. "James, we don't have a choice. He needs someone to take care of him."

"The courts—"

I cut him off. "You know as well as I do that the foster system isn't the best place for him. He needs to be with family. He's coming with us."

"You can't kidnap the kid." James sounds faraway as I squat back down and pick up the boy. He clings to me, and I gag at the smell, but I need to make my point to my husband. If that means picking the little boy up and holding him, even though the last thing I want to do is touch him, then I'll do that.

"It's not kidnapping," I argue, turning away from James and walking out the bedroom door. "We're saving him."

"You're kidnapping him," James argues, but I don't listen to him as I carry the boy out of the house and into the sunshine.

We're not kidnapping him. We're keeping him from a terrible life. I know better than anyone how rough the foster care system can be, and how terrible it can feel dealing with a mother who doesn't have it together enough to be a part of her child's life.

Camilla might be this boy's mother, but birthing a child doesn't mean you should be the one to take care of it.

This little boy is mine, and I'm going to do whatever it takes to keep him safe.

Nobody has to know what we did.

1

ELIZA

"Hold that pose for one more minute, Penelope," I say, tilting my phone just a little bit more to the right to try to capture the perfect shot. Penelope's still grinning at the camera like she has nothing better she'd like to be doing, but I can tell from the lines around her eyes that she's getting a little tired of sitting still for me. "I just need to make sure Clean Drinks can see their label in the shot."

After tapping the screen a few times to get a rapid-fire burst of photos, I finally exhale and nod at Penelope.

She groans, putting the drink down on the table and slipping from her seat. "Am I done? Can I go play now?"

I nod, hardly looking at her. These pictures are good. It's going to be tricky to pick the best one, which is a better outcome than what I thought was going to happen. The entire time I was shooting her, I was terrified I wasn't going to get a good enough shot, and then any money I'd get from Clean Drinks for their endorsed post would be the last I'd see from them.

This is it. This is the post that will make them want to

work with me long term. I've been building my platform for this, working hard to see it happen, and this one shot might be what will actually catapult me into making money more regularly.

My thumbs fly across the screen as I add the caption I thought out last night, then I hit post and slip my phone into my pocket. I'll update my blog later, but putting this picture up on Instagram will give my fans just enough of a taste to be really curious about what I'm doing.

"You look pleased about something." James walks into the dining room and wraps his arms around me.

I let him hug me for just a moment, but then my phone makes a trilling sound, and I wiggle away from him, pulling it out of my pocket.

"It was a good shot," I tell him, glancing up at him as I swipe on the screen. Twenty-three people have already liked my post, and the comments are rolling in. I watch them in real time, a flutter of excitement in my stomach with each one.

This is what James doesn't understand. It's thrilling to know that people aren't just looking at my posts, but that they *want* me to post. Why else would they like and comment on it so quickly? I have people out there just waiting to see what I'm going to do next, and companies are finally starting to pay attention.

"You took all morning to get that shot. Why don't you put the phone down now, and maybe we can do something as a family? It's nice out, and I thought we could set up the kiddie pool—"

I cut him off, knowing full well how much he hates it. "I need to be around to respond to any questions I might get about Clean Drinks. It doesn't do me any good to showcase how delicious they are, if I can't be around to answer questions, does it?"

He sighs and scrubs his hand down his face, but doesn't respond.

"Besides," I say, pushing him a little bit harder, so I will get the response I want, "we can go outside with Penelope, but you know as well as I do that the Millers have been living on their back deck this summer. What if they saw Knox?"

Again he sighs.

"You and I agreed that if we did this—"

"We'd do everything we could to keep him out of sight. I know that, Eliza." There's a sharp edge to his voice that I don't really like, but I know pointing it out isn't going to help anything. "I just don't think it's fair to keep him cooped up in the house all the time when Penelope's allowed to go outside and play whenever she wants."

As if on cue, I catch sight of our daughter streaking past the windows. She has a butterfly net in her hand and is chasing down some poor creature.

"If we let anyone know that we have him, then we'll lose him," I tell James, taking a step closer to him. In my hand, my phone keeps trilling and vibrating. It takes all of my self-control to stare at my husband and not check my notifications. "You agreed. You said that we were in this together. Keeping him safe is the most important thing. That means keeping him away from people who might tell."

He's silent. The way his jaw works tells me that he's thinking something, but that he's not yet sure what to say. It doesn't matter.

I turn away from James and turn on my phone's screen. There isn't anything he can say to make me change my mind. If we want to keep Knox, then we make sure nobody knows we have him.

That was the agreement.

Now it's time for me to see what all of my followers have to say about my post. If it gets enough traction, then I bet

Clean Drinks will want to hire me again. I might even be able to get them to sign a deal for multiple posts. They came to me because all of my shots are perfectly curated, designed to be beautiful, free from any clutter in the background.

It's the only way to keep the truth hidden.

It's the only way to keep Knox hidden.

2

BETHANY

"God, can you imagine having such a perfect life?" Even I can hear the envy dripping from my words as I turn my phone around to show Eliza Sullivan's latest post to my co-worker, Cindy.

She barely glances at the phone. She's in the middle of putting on her little apron and tying it in the back so it's nice and tight and won't sag when she puts a pen and pad of paper in the front pocket.

"I don't see why you're so obsessed with her." Her tone isn't rude, but I still feel myself stiffen a little bit at her words. "I mean, she has a kid. You don't. She's married; you're not. She lives in a mansion, and you live—"

"In a crappy little apartment, I know. And yeah, we may not be anything alike, but don't you just want to be like that? Look, her nail polish perfectly matches her earrings and the necklace Penelope has on."

Cindy pauses, a notepad in one hand, her pen in the other. "Who's Penelope?"

"Her daughter." Cindy doesn't respond, and I almost feel like I need to defend my fascination with Eliza. "Listen, I know the chances are good that we'd never ever be friends in real life, but it would be awesome. Can you imagine? Two summers ago, they flew to Maui for a week and took Penelope. I could go with them sometime. I'd be like an au pair, and Eliza's friend. It would be perfect. Before you say anything, you need to know that I've got it all planned out."

"Riiiight." She draws the word out as she shoves the pad and pen into her pocket. "I'm sure they'd love to have you tag along. How many shifts here do you think you'd have to work to pay for your flight over there? That's not even including lodging and food and all of the flowers you showed me they put in their hair."

I know I shouldn't let Cindy get me down, but it's hard not to feel a little disappointed. She's right, I'm sure of it, but when I look around the Tipsy Cat, I can't help but wish that I were anywhere but here. It didn't have to be Maui. Just someplace where my feet didn't stick to the floor when I walked around taking drink orders.

"Besides," Cindy says, her voice dragging me out of my calculations about how quickly I could squirrel away the money I'd need to go on a trip with Eliza and her family, "I bet she has tons of friends. Her summer vacation is probably already planned, and the first-class seats fill up quickly." She flips her blonde hair at me over her shoulder, then turns, sashaying through the swinging doors to the main seating area.

I watch her go, then cinch my own apron tightly around my waist. Even though there's part of me that's sure she's right that Eliza and I wouldn't ever be close friends... who's to say? Opposites attract, and all that.

And besides, even though I don't have the amount of money that they seem to, and even though our lives are vastly different, that doesn't mean we aren't similar on the inside. Isn't that what really matters?

Eliza's always posting inspirational quotes about loving who you are, and accepting others for who they are on the inside, when she's not busy posting perfect pictures of sandwiches for picnics with Penelope or cute little themed parties she throws. She might have money and fashion sense, but that doesn't mean she wouldn't want to be friends with me.

I know she would.

I just have to show her how close the two of us could be. Her entire life is perfect, and mine isn't, but I bet that being close to her and getting to spend time with her family and friends would rub off on me. I don't have family, and outside of work, I don't really have friends. My family wrote me off a long time ago, and I've always struggled with finding the right person to be friends with.

Until now.

Cindy would only laugh at me, which is why I couldn't ever tell her my plan or the fact that I've already started taking steps to make it come true. Eliza and I live in the same town; that much is obvious from the coffee shops she posts from when she's getting a latte with a little heart drawn in the foam, and from the parks she goes to when she wants to take pictures of her and Penelope on a weekend picnic.

It hasn't taken me very long to figure out her schedule. That's the cool thing about Eliza and yet another reason why we'd be friends. Once she's got a routine that she likes, she doesn't like to stray from it.

Glancing down at my watch, I grin to myself. Sure, I have a long eight-hour shift this afternoon and into the evening, and then I'm going to be exhausted when I head to Cool Beans bright and early in the morning... but Eliza stops by there every Saturday morning for a caramel latte at eight. I plan on running into her.

I just know we're going to be best friends.

She'll know it soon, too.

3

ELIZA

Saturday morning has got to be my favorite morning in the week. Not only is James home from the hospital, but he always keeps an eye on the kids so I can do some yoga, go get a latte, and then hit up Target for a little shopping.

Do I need anything from Target? No, I do not.

Has that ever stopped me? Also no.

James might not make a ton of money working as a doctor at a small county hospital, but that's fine, because his parents left him a small fortune when they died. As an only child, he got it all. They're the reason we have our gorgeous home, why James and I both drive brand-new cars, and why I never buy secondhand clothes.

His income is enough to keep our family afloat, but still, being able to pay for my own lattes with money from my blog is more than a little exciting. I started my blog, Penelope and Me, when I had just found out I was pregnant with her. It wasn't that I wanted to connect with other people online, but rather that I thought it would be a good way for me to remember everything that happened during my pregnancy and after Penelope was born.

For the longest time I never had any readers, but I kept telling myself that it was okay, that I wasn't doing it for other people. Then, one day completely out of the blue, a post I made about painting a dresser for Penelope's nursery went viral. I went from an average of five unique visitors a week to more than five thousand and realized that people didn't just want to hear about my trips to get an ultrasound.

They wanted to get intimate, personal. When Penelope was born, I posted about my leaky boobs when she had trouble breastfeeding, what it was like taking her to the store for the first time, and the cute little hair bows I made her so people would know that my bald baby was a little girl.

It was a balance to learn how to show everything personal in my life and still keep it all pretty and perfect, but I figured it out.

Instagram became a thing, and I hopped on it, happy to show little snapshots of my life, and people ate it up. It was easy to curate each little square to show my followers just how amazing my life is, and they love it. I've been written about by other blogs, linked to from news stations, and finally started getting brand sponsors just a few months ago.

And through it all, I've done everything I possibly can to keep Knox out of the limelight. None of my followers know I have him. They only know Penelope, with her perfect pigtails and the cutest smile, which I hope will help me win more sponsors. Everyone knows that companies love cute kids to hold their products, and that's why I had her pose with Clean Drinks earlier this week.

Speaking of which... I stop outside my favorite coffee shop and pull my phone from my pocket to check and see how well that post has done. It's not my top-liked one, which I'm sure the company won't be thrilled about, but I can't help it when my fans would rather see a video of Penelope jumping in the pool or of me showing off my new manicure.

Turning, I snap a quick selfie, making sure there isn't anyone in the background who might take away from how good I look, then post it with a coffee emoji and heart.

There.

As long as I keep posting regularly, then that will drive more people to my Instagram, which means more of them can find my website, which will mean...

"Eliza?"

The woman standing in front of me breaks my concentration, and I can't help but frown at her as I put my phone back in my purse, making sure to zip the top up. You can never be too careful, not when you have a very public job, like I do.

"I'm Eliza." I flash her a huge smile. "Do I know you?"

"Bethany," the woman says, grinning right back at me like the two of us are long-lost friends. "I follow your blog and recognized you from there. Doesn't this place just have the best lattes?"

She's shorter than me, and her eye makeup is a little heavy, a little amateur. What she needs to do is spend some time in front of the mirror in her bathroom to really work on making sure that she looks her best before she leaves the house, but I'm not going to tell her that. One bad minute of press could bring down everything that I've worked so hard for, so instead I nod, pull open the door to the coffee shop, and gesture for her to walk in.

"Their caramel lattes are so good," I gush, letting her lead me up to the counter. "I love coming here every Saturday and getting one. It's such a nice way to start out the weekend."

"Same." She smiles again and then turns to the girl at the counter to order. While she places her order for a small skim hazelnut latte, I check her out, taking in her cheap purse, the fact that the bottoms of her pants are torn from her stepping on them, how her belt is looking a little worn out in the back.

She's nice, but she's nothing like me, and she certainly isn't the type of person I want my brand to be associated with. I watch as she pays with dollar bills and drops fifty cents into the tip jar. When it's my turn, I make sure to put a five-dollar bill inside, tapping it in slowly so I can be sure she sees.

If you can't afford to tip, then you shouldn't go out.

"Want to sit with me?" Bethany has her latte and turns back to me, grinning as she points at a table for two in the corner of the coffee shop. "I love coming here and meeting new people."

That's absolutely the last thing I want to do. Coming to the coffee shop is supposed to give me time by myself, time to sit and scroll through social media, to think up new blog posts, to comment on other people's blogs so they'll reach out to me later. I really don't want to sit with someone I don't know and pretend to enjoy her company.

But what can I do? She's staring at me like she can't wait for my answer, and since she knows who I am, I don't think I have much of a choice. Besides, being nice to her just this once shouldn't be a problem. We'll both go our separate ways, and then I doubt I'll ever see her again.

"I'd like that," I lie, brushing past her to sit at a table by the window. I make sure to get the good seat so I can look out at the outdoor patio, not the one that will have me looking into the parking lot.

"It's just so cool to run into you here," she says, putting her latte down. I notice that there isn't any latte art in her foam, while mine has a pretty swirl and a heart.

It's probably because I'm such a good tipper.

"Yeah, I like coming here," I say, taking a sip of my latte. "So what do you do, Bethany?"

"I'm a cocktail waitress." The answer spills out of her. "It's not nearly as fun as what you do, but I'm thinking about starting a blog. You're just really inspiring, and you make your life look so perfect and beautiful. And your accent. I love it. Canadian?" She breathes out the words and stares at me.

Whoa.

I knew I had fans who followed every move I made and who ate up every word I typed out, but it's crazy to meet someone who likes me and what I do this much in person. Bethany is the first fan I've met in person, and I have to say... I love it.

"Thank you. And yes, I'm originally from Canada." I take a sip of my latte and smile at her. "I have a great life, trust me. James and Penelope make it so easy to come up with posts; I love being a mother and wife more than anything. Sounds like your life is pretty incredible, too."

She shakes her head. "It's not nearly as great as yours." Then, like someone has just reminded her she has something else to do, she glances down at her watch and then stands. "It was lovely to meet you, Eliza. I'm sure we'll run into each other again. Can't wait to be friends!"

She's gone before I can tell her that it was nice to meet her too, but that I'm not really looking for friends. Not that it matters; the city we live in is big enough that she'd have to actively search me out to bump into me regularly.

She's a little strange, but nothing's wrong with that. Pulling my cell phone out from my purse, I check my latest selfie, happy to see so many likes on it.

As I watch, a new comment pops up.

It's from Bethany.

Can't wait to see you again soon!

4

BETHANY

I can't believe that I finally got to run into Eliza. Of course, the blogger I admire so much can never know that I orchestrated the whole thing and that I've been planning to run into her for a while. I don't know how she'd react, but there's part of me that worries she might not take it as well as I'd want her to.

Then again, she's the one sharing every intimate detail of her life on her social media. If she didn't want someone to find her and try to connect with her, then maybe she should rethink how much personal information she shares.

That thought buoys me as I walk to my car in the parking lot. It's a junker, and I have to say a small prayer every time I crank the engine, in the hopes that it's going to start right up without any problems. Today seems to be my lucky day. The engine growls to life, startling a young mother and child walking by, and I give them an apologetic smile and a wave.

They don't return it.

Scowling, I pull out of the parking lot. As much as I'd love to stay and spend all morning talking with Eliza, I know better than to force myself on her right off the bat. We're going to be great friends, I know that we are, but that doesn't mean it's going to happen right away. I want it to feel more organic.

Cranking the radio, I roll down my window and blast some '80s music as I drive back to my apartment. I need to get to the laundromat today and make sure my uniform is clean for tonight. I also need to pop by the grocery store, get gas in my car, and swing by the post office to pay some bills.

So as much as I'd like to have sat and continued to talk and connect with Eliza, that just wasn't going to happen. It's fine, though; we both have very busy lives. It's good, actually, for her to see that I have things to do, too, so she doesn't think I'm going to just hang on her all the time.

An excited squeal escapes my lips as I pull into a parking space in front of my apartment building. It worked. I finally got to meet Eliza.

The thrill I feel over getting to talk to her and spend some time with her actually manages to cancel out the frustration I feel about where I live. My apartment building is on the bad side of town. Grass grows in cracks in the sidewalk, and someone always seems to be yelling at night, but it's home. Still, I'm really hoping I can find somewhere new to live before Eliza and I start to hang out.

That's something else I can put on the list for today: clean up my apartment. All of the money I've been saving from my job should be more than enough to help me buy some nicer furniture to make this place somewhere I'll be proud to bring Eliza back to hang out.

Unless I can get her to let me move in.

The thought stops me in my tracks; I shiver with excitement. That's a much better option than looking for a new place by myself. When Eliza and I are best friends, of course she'll want to help me out.

She can do that by giving me a great place to live.

I let myself in to my apartment, shake some food in my fish's bowl, and quickly gather up the laundry from my bedroom and bathroom. Had I been a little more organized this morning, I would have taken it with me to meet Eliza at the coffee shop. But I was just so excited that today was going to be the first day of our friendship that I didn't think about it.

It takes two trips, but I get all my laundry in the car, grab everything I need to go to the post office, and lock the door after myself. I'm halfway out to my car when I hear a little ding from my purse. I stop, dropping everything, to rummage through my purse and pull out my phone.

Maybe Eliza posted something about how amazing it was to meet a new friend for coffee this morning.

Maybe she saw my comment on her post and sent me a message or a friend request.

It's so exciting to think that someone as perfect as her might really want to be my friend that my finger shakes a bit as I swipe on my screen and tap on the notification. It's from Instagram, and my heart starts beating even faster.

Then my heart drops.

Cindy.

My co-worker posted a picture from our shift earlier this week, tagging me in it and writing a sappy caption about how cool it is to work with people you really like. I scowl, squinting as I look at the picture on the screen.

There's no way that I look like anyone Eliza would want to be friends with in real life. My hair is sweaty and slicked back away from my face so I can take orders and deal with customers without having to mess with my hair. And there's a stain on the front of my shirt from where a drunk guy spilled his drink on me. And I look... exhausted.

My mascara has made shadows under my eyes, and I cringe, immediately looking for a way I can remove the tag so Eliza won't see this picture of me. The last thing I want is for her to get home from the coffee shop, decide to add me on Instagram, and then somehow see this. It's so unlike her, such a juxtaposition to her perfect life, that I want to delete it and make sure nobody ever sees it.

"Come on, Cindy," I mutter, fumbling with my phone. I finally figure out how to remove the tag and sigh with relief, then decide to hop over to Eliza's profile, just to see if she updated again.

Unfortunately, no. The most recent post is still just her selfie from outside the coffee shop.

She really is beautiful. Everything about her life is perfect; I can't wait to be a part of it. Just being friends with her will be enough for me. I don't want to take her husband, don't want to take over her life.

I'm not crazy.

I just want her as my friend.

Today was just the start of our friendship, and I'm patient. Eliza didn't get the perfect life and perfect family by letting just anyone get close to her, so I understand if she's a little cautious about who she wants to be friends with.

But I'm persistent.

That's the thing everyone says about me. I've always taken it to heart.

When I really want something, I'm willing to do whatever it takes to get it.

And I want to be friends with Eliza.

5

ELIZA

I have to read the email that just landed in my inbox three times before I'm sure that I know what it says, and before I can trust the fact that the words aren't going to change or delete themselves when I look away.

"James." I call my husband without looking up from my phone screen. "James, come here."

He's in the house somewhere; I know that much. After I got home from the coffee shop, he went outside to putter around the yard with Penelope, leaving me with Knox, but I know I heard the door open and close again. My screen dims, and I tap it to wake it back up before looking up from my phone.

Penelope's in front of me, a smile on her face, gripping the hem of her dress and waving it back and forth a little bit.

"Can I have some ice cream?" She bats her eyes at me—a trick she learned to use on her father to get whatever she wanted—and then continues, "And Knox, too. I'm sure he'd want some."

"Knox is napping," I tell her, but just then I hear him start to cry over the baby monitor I have set up on the kitchen counter. I never thought I was going to use the things when I had children, but our house is so big I can't hear him without it.

"Okay, fine," I say, putting my phone down and standing up. "Get out the bowls and spoons, but I'm in charge of scooping. Do you know where your dad is?"

"Outside in the roses." Penelope throws the words at me over her shoulder as she hurries over to the cupboard. "He said to ask you about ice cream."

"Of course he did," I mutter to myself, hurrying from the kitchen. "Just when I need him, he's busy." By the time I get to Knox's room, his soft crying has escalated, and he's standing in his crib, his little fists grabbing the side of it, his mouth open in a wail.

Wincing at the sound, I scoop him up and nuzzle against him, giving him a kiss on the cheek. "Knoxy boy, I'm here, I'm here. Did you have a good nap?"

He settles down immediately and blinks up at me, giving me time to reach out and wipe the tears away from his eyes. They're startling blue, just like Camilla's, and at first it unnerved me a little bit to look into his eyes and see my sister there.

To be honest, at first a lot of things unnerved me. I couldn't help the fact that both James and I jumped every time someone came to the house. For the first month after we brought Knox home with us, I thought for sure that anyone at the door would be a police officer. I was terrified that Camilla would have gotten herself together enough to look for him, and that she would, somehow, know that we had taken him.

Of course, those fears were ridiculous. Camilla loves nothing more than she loves pumping herself full of drugs. I wonder sometimes if she even remembers having a little boy. It wouldn't surprise me if she woke up once, tried to remember if she had a son, then convinced herself it had all been a fever dream or a hallucination.

Of course, I found out later that she did get it together. A few months after bringing Knox home, I looked online for news reports of missing kids and found one involving Camilla. She got sober long enough to miss him and file a report, then disappeared again. I doubt she even considered the possibility that James and I could have taken him.

It was about a year and a half ago that we took Knox, and even though I think he's probably around three by now, he still naps every afternoon and doesn't talk nearly as much as Penelope did when she was his age.

No, scratch that. He hardly talks at all.

It's just another thing that I fully blame my sister for. If she had been a more involved mother, if she hadn't done drugs while she was pregnant with him, if she had just read him a book once in his life...

I shake my head and take a deep breath. Getting angry with my little boy in my arms isn't going to solve anything. I need to remain present in the moment. Knox is here, with us, with the family that he deserves, and Camilla won't ever get him back.

"Penelope and I are scooping out ice cream," I tell him, kissing him on the forehead. I'm rewarded with a grin, and I laugh as he wiggles out of my grasp and then hurries out of the room, only glancing back at me once to make sure I'm following. What he needs to do is try to pee and then go downstairs, but seeing Knox happy makes me happy, and I'm willing to risk a little accident with him today.

Besides, I have great news to tell James. There really isn't anything that can ruin my day right now.

By the time Knox and I get into the kitchen, Penelope has everything set up for the two of them to eat ice cream, including a box of sprinkles I had wedged in a cupboard next to the fridge and some chocolate syrup. I scoop them each a bowl, watching as Penelope carefully doctors up the chocolate ice cream for both of them; then I put everything away while they start to eat.

"Keep an eye on Knox, and try to get him to pee when you two are done, okay? You're such a big helper," I say, kissing Penelope on the top of her head before scooping my phone up from the kitchen table and walking outside to find James. He's told me a few times that it's not fair to expect Penelope to help out so much with Knox, because she's only six, but she really loves spending time with him, and right now, I need to talk to my husband.

Like our daughter said, he's in the roses, trimming away, a smile on his face.

"Hey, you," I say, picking up a fallen bloom and sniffing it before letting it drop out of my hand. "It's looking really good out here."

"You think so?" Pausing to wipe his brow, James grins at me and then takes a step back to get a better look at what he's done. "I noticed yesterday before dinner that this rose bush was looking a little out of control and thought I could do something about it."

"It's great," I tell him, then wait a moment before continuing, "Hey, I have really good news."

This gets his attention, just like I knew it would. James is always supportive of anything I have going on, which is one of the things I love so much about him. When he's looking at me, I pause just for a moment, for dramatic effect, then tell him what I wanted to say before Knox woke up from his nap and Penelope wanted ice cream.

"Another brand reached out to me. They said they've been watching me for a while, and they like how I connect with my followers and the persona that I've built online. They want—get this—not just one post, but two a week. For a month." I wave my phone in the air between us like he's going to be able to see the email.

"Really? Eliza, that's great." James closes the gap between us and pulls me in for a hug. "You must be over the moon."

"I am." It feels like I touched an electric wire, I'm so excited right now. "This is what I've been working so hard for, James. I knew I could do it, could build a platform where companies wanted to work with me, and I've done it! They didn't tell me yet how much they want to pay, but all money is good money." I flash him a grin.

"What company is it? What kind of posts do they want you to do? I know you were really concerned about staying true to the brand you had made." He pulls back and searches my face for an answer.

"True Green," I say, but the expression on his face doesn't change. That's fine; James doesn't pay attention to the cleaning supplies available in the store, not when I'm so willing to do all of the shopping for our family. "They're an eco-friendly company using all-natural ingredients that are kid- and pet-safe."

"We have the kid part of that down pat. Do they know or care that we don't have a pet?"

I shrug. "I'm not sure. Of course, now could be the time to get a dog." It's a discussion we've had a hundred times, but James always puts his foot down about it. I think nothing would help my blog more than a puppy in some of the pictures, but he doesn't see it that way. "Like a golden retriever or a goldendoodle. Both of those would look great in my posts."

He laughs, but grows serious as he reaches out and takes my hands in his. "Eliza, I'm really happy for you, you know that," he says, and I feel a chill run through me at the sudden change in his demeanor. "I just want you to make sure you're doing the right thing. I know your blog is taking off, but we don't need the money, not really. And you need to think about Knox—"

"I do think about him." It feels rude, but I pull my hands from his grasp. "You think that I wasn't thinking about him when we saved him from that drug house he was living in?"

James shakes his head. "Eliza, Knox isn't ours. I know we took him, but someone is going to find out eventually. What in the world are you going to do then?"

"How would they find out?" I'm angry now, and I take a deep breath to try to calm myself back down. "The only way they'd find out is if someone told, and Penelope knows she can't."

"We need to think about taking him back, or—"

"We're not taking him back. He's our son."

James grows frustrated. I can see it in the red splotches appearing in his cheeks and how he scrubs his hand down his face. When we were dating, I thought it was so sexy when he did that. Now, though, I know that it just means he's really frustrated with me.

"He's our nephew. He has no life, Eliza, not just living in the house all the time because we're both afraid to let him out where someone might see him. What if you make a mistake? What if you post a picture and he's in it? You need to think about giving him back to Camilla, or giving up the blogging. I didn't like it then, and now I'm even more worried it's all going to backfire on us."

"Giving up the blogging? Are you serious? I'm finally making it, James! Companies want to work with me; they want me to represent them. They reach out to me. I'm not giving that up, and I'm certainly not giving up Knox. I'm keeping him—we're keeping him. I'll homeschool him if I need to, but I'm not sending him back to my sister to rot in that drug house. No way. I'm not changing anything."

He opens his mouth to respond, but I'm too angry to

stand here and listen to what he has to say, so I spin away from him, stalking back to the house. James thinks I can't have it all, but he's wrong. I'm going to have it all, and I'm not changing a single thing about my life.

It's perfect just the way it is.

Nothing is going to change that.

6

BETHANY

I don't get a chance to run into Eliza again until the middle of the next week. One of the girls at the bar where I work quit, and while it's been great having her extra income flowing into my pocket, I haven't really enjoyed how much more time I'm spending at work. Even though I'd much rather be doing most anything other than serving cocktails to drunk men with wandering hands, now that I'm standing in front of Target with extra cash in my purse, I can't help but be a little grateful for the extra shifts I had to pick up.

I'll never have as much money as Eliza does, but that's fine. I don't need as much income as she has to show her how close of friends we can really be. I'm a bit nervous walking in here to buy something for full price, since all of my clothes and accessories come from thrift shops, but Eliza posted on Sunday about this darling purse she bought at Target, and I want one.

Holding my head high, I walk into the store, my eyes flicking around me as I go to look for Eliza. She blogged about how going to Target was her personal treat to herself, and that she was going to be stopping in every evening this week, to check their spring collection for clothes to go with her new purse.

Obviously I'm not going to buy a new dress or shoes, but I can handle the purse. I downloaded a coupon onto my phone and counted out the money I need last night so I'd be prepared when I made it in this morning.

At the purse section, I see what I want. The light pink crossbody isn't what I would have chosen for myself. Normally I'd choose a black one so that it'd go with the rest of my clothes, but Eliza chose a pink one, so that's what I'm going to wear. It would be silly of me to get excited, make the trip, and then spend my money on the wrong purse.

The fake leather feels buttery in my hands, and I take a sniff of it, pleased with the sterile smell. Unlike my other purses, it doesn't smell like cigarettes, alcohol, or just plain sweat. It will be really nice to have something new for myself for once. I tuck it under my arm to see how it will feel.

"I just bought that one," a cheery voice behind me says, and I feel my pulse spike. I'd know Eliza's voice anywhere from the livestreams and videos she posts, and I slap a huge smile on my face as I turn around to greet her.

"Hey!" My voice is cheery and bright.

Did her face just fall a little bit? No, surely not. Not when we've already met once, and I'm so sure we're going to be good friends. She's probably just surprised to be so lucky as to run into me again so soon after we first met, that's all. There's no reason why she would look at all disappointed about seeing me.

"It's a great color," Eliza says, and even though she still sounds friendly, I can't help but think there's a little ice behind the words. Penelope peers out from behind her mother's legs, dressed in a perfect spring dress and cute sandals.

"Hi, Penelope," I say, smiling at the girl and giving her a half-wave. "Are you having fun out with your mom?"

"Yes." Penelope smiles back, then glances up at Eliza for direction. Poor girl doesn't yet know how to handle having a mom as well known as Eliza is, but I'm sure she'll get better at it. After all, Eliza has her in practically all of her Instagram posts, and Penelope always looks like she's enjoying herself.

"I'm Bethany," I say, looking back at Eliza. "We met at the coffee shop on Saturday, remember?"

"Sure do. You must have seen my post about how great this pink color is, right? Is that why you're here?" Eliza tilts her head to the side a little bit, like she's trying to read my mind.

I shake my head. It's a lie, and I hope she can't see that, but I suddenly don't want Eliza to know that I follow every minute detail of her life as closely as I really do. "No, I was just looking for a cute summer purse and saw it. The color is great and..." I try to remember what Eliza said about the purse. "I think it will look cute with my outfits."

Eliza smiles, but her mouth still seems tight. "Good choice, and how lucky that you were able to get the last one. Now, it's nice to see you again, but Penelope and I have some shopping to do. Goodbye, Bethany."

"Wait!" Without thinking, I drop the purse back down onto the display and follow Eliza and Penelope out from the purse section. "I had such a nice time with you at the coffee shop this weekend that I wanted to know if you wanted to make it a date sometime. I think we'd have a lot of fun."

There's a pregnant pause. This is the moment I've been hoping for, my chance to finally talk to Eliza, and show her that the two of us are meant to be friends. Penelope shifts position next to her mother, but neither of them say anything.

"That's lovely of you, Bethany, really," Eliza finally says, and I feel so excited I start to smile before she has a chance to say anything else.

"Great, I was thinking I could meet you there on Saturday," I begin, but Eliza isn't finished talking yet.

"But I'm just so busy right now that I'm not looking for a commitment like that. Have a great day, though. It was lovely to run into you again." She wiggles her fingers at me, then throws me a megawatt smile before tugging Penelope away. The little girl glances over her shoulder once to look at me; then the two of them are swept up in a group of women descending on a rack of summer dresses.

"What just happened?" I whisper the question to myself, unsure of whether I should follow her and try to get her to talk to me, to see that we really could be friends if she would give it a chance, or if I should walk away.

Even though it's not what I want to do, I decide to walk away.

For now.

My face burns, and my steps feel heavier than they've ever felt as I work my way back to the purses. The pink crossbody bag that I had in my hands a moment ago so I would match Eliza seems ridiculous now, like something that will only mock me when I wear it, but I still want it.

I'm going to prove to Eliza that the two of us should be friends, and there's just no way that I can expect to do that if she doesn't see that I'm equal in some ways.

Stopping in front of the display where I left the purse, I glance around for it, then look harder, lifting black and brown purses to move them out of the way while I look for sight of the creamy pink.

It's not here.

"You've got to be kidding me," I say to myself, catching the attention of a woman who's also digging through the purses. I glance over at her. "Did you happen to see a pink crossbody in here? I set it down and then changed my mind that I want it, but I don't see it."

Her eyes widen a bit. I look past her to her cart, where the purse is nestled on top of a stack of clothes, in between boxes of crackers and cookies.

"That's it. That's my purse." Without thinking about what I'm doing, I push past her, reaching out for the purse.

"That's mine. I'm buying it for my daughter." She steps to the side, quickly blocking my path. "You'll have to choose another purse. That one is already taken."

"No, you don't understand." I take another step, but she moves faster than I do, somehow keeping her body in between me and the cart. "I really need that purse. It's the last one like that. I have to have it."

She doesn't get it. She has no way of understanding that if I'm going to become friends with Eliza, that I don't just want that purse—I *need* it. I have to become Eliza's friend. To do that, I have to show her that we're more alike than she seems to think.

"I'm buying that purse." The woman's voice is firm, her eyes slits. "If you try to take it out of my cart, then the two of us are going to have a problem."

Someone walking by pauses and looks at the two of us.

My face, already red, feels like it's going to burst into flames. I hate feeling like everyone is looking at me and judging me, but that's exactly what's happening right now.

"Fine," I say. "Keep the purse."

It kills me to walk away from the purse, but I'll figure out another way to get Eliza to like me. She doesn't know that the two of us are going to be friends, but I do.

Eliza is going to be my best friend. No matter what.

7

ELIZA

I get home from Target feeling a little frazzled. All I want is a cup of tea and to sit in the backyard for a few minutes while the birds sing, but I still need to make dinner and get the kids their baths before updating my blog with a new post.

James greets me at the door, Knox in his arms, and I push past him, slamming the front door shut as quickly as possible.

"So nice to have you two greet me at the door," I say, making sure there's a smile on my face, "but we need to be really careful that nobody sees Knox."

James inhales hard before he speaks. "Nobody was going to see him," he says, putting Knox down so he can chase after Penelope. "Everyone on the street is having dinner, and besides, we could always say we were watching a nephew or something. That should have been the story we went with from the beginning."

"This is not a conversation I want to have," I say, dropping my shopping bags on the floor and walking into the kitchen. I'm expecting to have to start a meal from scratch, so I'm pleasantly surprised to see a pizza cooling on the stove, the table already set with two places. "You made dinner?" I turn to James, wanting him to see how happy I am.

"For the kids. I thought the two of us could talk." Before I can respond, he turns and yells for the kids to come to dinner. They fly in, and we get them settled; then James takes me by the hand and leads me out onto the back porch, making sure to close the French doors behind us.

"This sounds serious," I joke, but inside I feel my stomach twist. "You made dinner for the kids, which is awesome, but I can't help but feel like I did something wrong."

"We need to talk about Knox." As soon as the words are out of his mouth, I feel myself start to shut down. James knows that I don't want to have a conversation about him, and here he is, bringing it up right when I get home from the most stressful Target trip ever.

"You mean our son?" Crossing my arms, I turn in my chair to look at him. "What do you want to talk about?"

"He's not ours, Eliza, and you know it. He's a great kid, but he needs help. He doesn't talk; I know you see that. You can't keep him in the house all the time like this. What are we going to do when it's time for him to go to school?"

I frown. "I told you, I'm going to homeschool him."

"And you're never going to take him on field trips?" I don't answer, so he continues, "You and I can keep a secret, but what about Penelope? What are you going to do if she slips up at school this fall and tells everyone that we have a little boy in our house who isn't really ours?"

"She won't. She knows how important this is. Besides, James, I thought you were on board with this. We were both there when we took him, remember?" I want to yell at my husband, and I have to fight to keep my voice down so the kids don't hear us. Glancing over my shoulder, I'm pleased to see the two of them still digging into their meal.

"It was a mistake." James sighs. "You know as well as I do that we shouldn't have taken him."

"Yeah, and what do you think we should have done? Left him there to rot in that house with Camilla?"

"We should have called the police," he says, but I'm already shaking my head.

"We went over this, James. The police would take him, send him to social services. He'd go into foster care, and who knows how he would end up then? We're his family. He needs us."

"He needs a normal childhood."

That one hurts, and I blink hard to keep from crying. James has to know that saying that to me, after Camilla and I grew up in foster care, would be more than enough to hurt me, yet he looked me right in the eyes and said it anyway.

"I'm giving him a normal childhood," I argue. "You have no idea how happy he is, because you're at work most of the time. Trust me, James, I wouldn't do anything that would hurt him. I love him." My voice breaks.

"I know you do," James says, reaching out and taking my hand. My first thought is to yank it back from his grasp, but I let him link his fingers through mine. "I know you love Knox. I just want to make sure we're giving him the best possible life."

"Believe me," I scoff. "What we're doing for him is worlds better than what would happen if we were to send him to foster care. There's just no comparison. We love him; he loves us. He's happy; he's safe. He doesn't have to worry about whether or not someone is going to get tired of him one day and just... send him back."

"Eliza." James sighs. "I know your childhood wasn't easy, and I don't want you to think that I don't believe you're doing everything in your power to take care of Knox, it's just that I want to make sure we're on the same page and that he has the best possible life."

"He *will*," I say, squeezing James' fingers. "He will, because we're going to give it to him. We both work so hard, and we play hard with him, and we both do whatever it takes to keep him happy and safe. Really, he couldn't ask for anything more. I think you know that."

There. That should be enough to get James to see how serious I am about keeping Knox. I never had anyone in my life advocating for me like we're doing for him, and there's no way I'm going to just sit back and watch as something terrible happens to him. He's my son—*our* son—and I'm going to do whatever it takes to keep him.

"Okay, I'm sorry I upset you," James tells me. "I do think we need to consider how we can help him more."

I disagree, but fighting with him right now is the last thing I want to do. Even though I believe him that he feels bad about our conversation just now, it's obvious that there's more he wants to say, but isn't ready to bring up.

"What else did you want to talk about?" I slip my fingers from his hand and brush hair back behind my ear, tucking it there as I try to look casual. He has to know that I'm a bundle of nerves right now, and that I feel like the floor has just dropped out from under me.

"It's your blogging," James says, and I feel my chest tighten. "I know you're careful to keep Knox off it, and I know how much you enjoy it, but it really doesn't bring in enough money for you to worry about it as much as you do. I want to talk about you spending more time focused on the kids, especially if you're going to homeschool Knox."

I feel trapped, like he made me tell him I want to homeschool Knox so he could use that as ammunition against me with my blogging. But instead of getting angry, I swallow hard and choose my words carefully.

"You know that contributing to the household has always been important to me," I begin, and he opens his mouth to speak, but I hold up a single finger to prevent him. "Hang on, James, let me finish this thought. I've always wanted to contribute *financially*, not just as a mother, and blogging allows me to do that while still keeping the house clean and taking care of the kids. I don't want to give it up. It's starting to take off. I'm getting more and more readers who really connect with what I'm saying."

"I know, and you do such a good job at it," James tells me. "I just think it's dangerous to be taking pictures around the house with Knox here, and that you could spend more time with the kids if you were to give it up. You could give him the attention and help he really needs."

"I'm not giving it up." My voice is hard, but I want to make sure he understands how important this is to me. "I've always supported you whenever you've come to me with a dream or plan you want to go for, James, and I really would appreciate it if you would support me in the same way."

"I do support you." He sounds exasperated and runs his hand through his hair.

"Then don't ask me to get rid of Knox or my blog again," I say, standing and walking away from him. I know it's rude to just leave the conversation like this, but I want to get inside, see the kids, get something to eat.

I'm a bit shaken, if I'm being honest with myself. Running into that woman at Target and dealing with her over-the-top desire to be friends, and then James pushing me to change what I'm doing is enough to make me feel like I'm coming out of my skin. Instead of letting it really get to me, though, I pose with Penelope and snap a picture with her, uploading it to Instagram without much thought.

Perfect evenings with this kiddo make all the hard work worth it.

There. My followers will eat that up. They love anything with Penelope in it. I don't often post candid shots, so this will be a real treat for some of them. Not only that, but it is a great way to show James how much people like reading what I have to say and connecting with me.

He can just get over himself, with asking me to give up Knox and my blogging.

Neither of those things are ever going to happen.

8

BETHANY

I can't help but cringe when I think about how upset Eliza seemed to be with me when I ran into her at Target a few days ago. It was obvious she didn't want to run into me there, but I can't believe that it's because she doesn't want to be friends.

She was frazzled.

She was on a mission.

She had Penelope with her.

All of those things add up to make it clear that I should have taken my time, tried to reach out to her when she was on her own and not in a hurry. I know I tend to come across a little pushy sometimes when there's something that I really want, but I can make sure she sees just how supportive a friend I can really be.

That's why I'm at the coffee shop early this morning. I beat her here and ordered us each a latte, making sure to tell the barista that one was for Eliza. They put a pretty little swirl on top of it, and I hoped they would do the same to mine, but it still just looks like a boring pour.

Whatever. I take a sip of it, wincing at how hot it is. If I drink from it a little bit, then chances are good that Eliza won't be able to tell that it didn't have latte art on the top. By the time she gets here to join me, it'll just look like I drank enough to mess up the art.

I'm going to make sure to take it a bit slower so I don't come across too eager for her friendship. I am—I definitely am—but sometimes you have to slow down for people so you don't scare them off.

"I can do this," I whisper to myself, taking another sip of my latte. Coffee really isn't my favorite, but Eliza loves it, so I'm going to do whatever I can to show her that we can do things together when we become friends. We can get coffee every Saturday, go shopping, maybe even go on vacation together.

I'd love to hang out with Penelope by the pool while she and James have a fancy dinner, if that's what she'd like. I'd be like her best friend and Penelope's honorary aunt, and I'd be willing to watch her for free.

"This is going to be perfect," I say, checking my watch. It's eight, which is right when Eliza gets her coffee every week. She's never late, not according to the posts she puts on Instagram of her pretty latte or her smiling face, and I'm mentally congratulating myself for getting here early enough to buy her drink when the door swings open.

Sure, buying two lattes isn't cheap, but after I missed out on that pink crossbody bag this week, I have a little extra money to spend. I realize I'm holding my breath when a woman walks through the door, but exhale quickly in disappointment when I realize it's not Eliza.

"Where are you?" She should be here by now, should be in line, laughing with the barista, getting her drink, coming to sit down at this table. I'm even at the table she likes best, the one with the great view, and I made sure to take the other seat so she could look out the window once she joined me.

It's all perfect, but she's not here.

I baby my latte, not wanting to finish it before she joins me, my head snapping up every time the door opens.

No Eliza.

It's been fifteen minutes. She's never this late, and I'm starting to worry that something may have happened to her or to Penelope. If her daughter is sick or she got in a fight with James, then she might not make it out to get coffee today. What she really needs is a friend there to take care of her.

If I knew where she lived, then I'd go there right now to offer my support. She'd be surprised to see me at her door, I'm sure of it, but she'd get over it quickly when she realized that I was there just to help her through whatever she's going through.

I'm that good a friend.

Pulling my phone from my old black purse, I swipe on the screen and navigate to her Instagram. If something came up, she might have made a post about it, but I doubt she'll have any personal information about Penelope if she's sick.

That's the only thing that makes sense. She loves coming out for her Saturday coffee, and I don't think she ever misses. It would have to be something really terrible to keep her from coming to her favorite coffee shop and getting something to drink.

Poor Penelope, not feeling well. It's so good of her mom to stay home with her instead of coming out for coffee, even though that does leave me with a latte I don't want to drink. If I knew where she lived, I'd just take the drink to Eliza.

It takes the page a minute to load, thanks to the spotty Wi-Fi in this coffee shop, but when it does, I feel a cold chill shiver through my body. There's a picture of Eliza holding a latte up, a huge grin on her face.

Turning in my seat, I look around for her.

She's not here, but then where is she?

My fingers tremble as I scroll up so I can read the caption under the picture.

"Decided to get out of my normal routine and try a new coffee shop this morning. Even when you're perfectly happy doing the same thing over and over again, it's important to try something new from time to time. Doing that is the only way to make sure that you're growing as a person, and to keep from getting stagnant. Who knows where I'll be next Saturday?"

My voice trails off when I finish reading the caption. There are a handful of emojis after the words, hearts and flowers, a little cup of coffee, and praying hands.

Behind her, in the window of the coffee shop, I can see the name of where she is. It's backwards, so it takes me a moment to decode, but I finally read it.

Kava Java.

"She didn't come here," I whisper to myself, dropping my phone on the table like it burned me. "Why would she go somewhere else without telling me that she was going to do that?"

My heart's beating so hard I can hear my pulse. It pounds in my ears, and I'm suddenly overwhelmed with all of the noise in the coffee shop.

How have I never before noticed just how loud this place is? The barista keeps calling out drink orders, families are here with little kids who are laughing and talking over each other... even the music piped in through the speakers in the ceiling is suddenly so loud I feel like I'm losing my mind.

"Excuse me," a woman says, and I look up at her, hope flowing through me that Eliza is going to be standing there talking to me. She smiles at me, and my heart falls when I take in her red pixie cut, the tattoos on her arms, the ring through her nose that makes her look like a bull.

Eliza would never.

"Are you finished with this table? My best friend and I need a place to sit." She gestures behind her with the cup she's holding. Again I feel nervous.

Is Eliza her best friend? Did she leave Kava Java and come here with this redhead just to make me feel bad?

Craning my neck to see behind the woman, I relax when I notice the person behind her isn't Eliza. I stare at her for a moment before I realize that I still haven't answered the redhead.

"I'm done," I mutter, grabbing both cups and standing up. "You can have it."

I feel like I'm walking through a dream as I wind through the busy coffee shop, avoiding little kids running around and doing my best not to kick any purses on the floor. When I reach the trash can, I toss in my cup, then realize that Eliza's drink is still full.

Do I drop it in the trash?

Do I pour it down the sink?

Turning around to see if anyone might be standing near me to offer me some advice, my heart sinks when I take in the scene. It's like I don't exist to these people. Even though I know it's going to make a mess for the employees later, I dump Eliza's full latte into the trash, then toss her cup in on top.

It's their fault she didn't come here today, so they should have to clean this up. If they'd done a better job making sure she got the perfect drink each Saturday, then she wouldn't have tried out a new coffee shop, and I would have been able to sit and hang out with my new friend.

Leaning against my car in the parking lot, I make sure to

like Eliza's new post; then I get behind the wheel, nosing out into traffic as I head across town.

Surely Eliza didn't mean to leave me on my own for coffee this morning. I'll just swing by the Kava Java and see if she's still there. We can still have a wonderful morning together.

I'm going to make sure of it.

9

ELIZA

This latte isn't nearly as good as the one that I normally get at Cool Beans, but I didn't want to run into Bethany there. It's not that I know for sure she was going to be there, but was it really worth the risk? She's kinda weird, really pushy, and I don't like how sure she is of the fact that the two of us are going to be close friends.

Because we're not.

If I were to have a really close friend, then they might, at some point, find out about Knox. I can't let that happen, which is why I like connecting with my readers and followers through social media. They never ask to get invited over to my house for dinner, and they certainly haven't ever just shown up in a place where I was going to be.

Until Bethany started doing just that.

A shiver runs down my spine. I finish my latte, crumple the cup in my hand, then throw it in the trash can by the door before heading out to my car. This was not the super relaxing morning that I wanted it to be. James mentioned again after breakfast how he thought I needed to reconsider my blogging and social media. I told him that it wasn't going to happen.

When I left the house to get my latte, I could feel how unhappy he was with me, but we both tried to keep a smile on our faces so Penelope and Knox didn't notice. Ever since we brought him home from Camilla's, I've done everything I can to make him feel like he's really our son, like he fits in with our family.

The last thing I want is for him to realize that we're hiding him away from the rest of the world. He has no idea about that right now, but one day he might.

I'm about to start my car when I have a brilliant idea for my next blog post. Instead of cranking the engine and heading back to the house, I pull a small notebook from my purse and click on my pen.

Scribbling down my ideas on a piece of paper like this isn't my favorite way to plan out blog posts, but when you're on the move, you have to do what you have to do. There's no way I'm going to try to remember this idea all the way home and risk forgetting it by the time I pull into the garage.

When faced with obstacles in your life, you can either bow to them and let them beat you, or you can pull yourself together and face them head-on. It's wonderful to have a partner in your corner who will do whatever it takes to help you out, but never be afraid to face things alone! As a mom, you already have the most important job, and one that tends to be thankless. There's no reason to ever feel like you can't handle whatever life throws your way.

I tap my pen against my chin and strike out the first two sentences. The last thing I need is for my readers to get an inkling that there's any friction between James and me. That's one of the reasons why I love the fact that I can always rewrite my work—I never accidentally leave in any upsetting information or anything that might lead my readers back to my family.

Make sure you remember just how powerful you are, moms! You not only birthed a child, you now are in charge of helping them grow and giving them the strength they need to face this world. You are stronger than any warrior and...

"This is crap," I mutter, flipping my notebook shut and throwing it into the seat next to me. It's almost impossible for me to write anything decent when I'm upset about something that happened at home, and this argument with James doesn't seem like it's going to die down anytime soon.

If he really thinks that I'm ever going to be willing to give Knox up, though, he's got something else coming to him. Knox is mine.

Nobody is going to take him from me.

And my blog is mine. I might not make nearly as much money as he does, but I love it, I touch people's lives, and I'm not giving up on it just because my husband thinks I might have trouble balancing it all.

"James has to back off and see that I can do it all," I mutter, cranking the engine and pulling out of the parking lot. I keep my eyes open, because there are tons of people milling about between the cars like they don't have anywhere better to be. This coffee shop isn't one that I want to come back to anytime soon, but I'm just going to have to see if I can find one that feels like home.

Or I just need to tell Bethany that she has to back off.

Wasn't I just writing down some drivel about moms being braver and stronger than warriors? If I can't look my fan in the face and tell her that I need some space, then what kind of an example am I being for Penelope?

Maybe Bethany won't be a problem in the future. She probably just saw me at the coffee shop last week and then got excited, then had it happen again at Target. As strange as that was for me, there's no reason for me to believe that it was anything other than her just getting overexcited.

Influencers can have that effect on people. Not everyone understands it, and while I'm certainly not famous by any stretch of the imagination, in certain circles of people, I definitely have fans.

That's all she is. A fan.

And if I get an inkling that she may be more or if I think for a second that she's at all creepy, then I'll just tell her to back off. She's a grown woman, and I can't imagine her getting really offended if I told her that I wasn't in the market for new friends.

Bethany's obnoxious, like a fly, but that doesn't mean she's dangerous. I know I have a tendency to overanalyze things and daydream about situations that won't ever happen, and that's probably what's going on here.

If I see her again, I'll tell her to back off.

But I doubt I will. She has her own life to live. I'm sure she has friends.

What in the world would make her think that she had to be mine?

10

BETHANY

I'm just walking over to Eliza's car to knock on her window and tell her that I'm happy to see her when she buckles her seatbelt, throws the car into drive, and zips out of the parking lot like she's in a mad rush to get somewhere.

For just a moment I stand completely still, shocked to see her drive away so quickly, but when she gets held up by a group of teenagers on skateboards by the parking lot exit, I run back to my car, my purse slapping into my side, and follow her.

I'm buzzing with excitement, and I turn down my radio, finally clicking it off so I can concentrate on where Eliza's going. She drives quickly, and I cut off a minivan so I can stay behind her. When they honk, I give them a friendly little wave to let them know that I'm sorry, then press down harder on the gas to keep up.

Hopefully she doesn't drive this fast with Penelope in the car, but I have to admit that I like how quickly Eliza's driving. It makes it feel like the two of us are on an adventure as we fly around curves and zip around corners on her way home.

At least, I hope that's where she's going. If she's going to a store, then I'm going to have to come up with a reason to be at the same one, and judging by the posts she's made after grocery shopping, she probably shops at the ritzy stores I can't afford.

Then again, if she is going home, I can't exactly hop out and tell her how happy I am to see her. She might construe it as creepy, and that's the last thing I want. After our run-in at Target, I need to make sure I don't come on too strong.

That's why I went to Cool Beans this morning. I thought that meeting her there and buying her a drink would be a great way to show her how similar the two of us really are, without showing up somewhere she might not expect me. No, I don't have a family like she does, and I definitely don't have as much money as she does, but we're the same deep down.

I just know it.

It's only when we pull into a fancy neighborhood with large stone walls at the front entrance that I realize I'm holding my breath. I exhale hard, loosening up my grip on the steering wheel. As much as I'd like to pull into Eliza's driveway right behind her, I need to make sure to keep my distance so she doesn't look in her rearview mirror and wonder who's stopping by unannounced.

Letting off the gas, I force myself to allow her to pull ahead of me. It's not like she's going to suddenly pull a U-turn and drive away from me, so I can afford to let her drive farther ahead if that's what it takes to keep her from knowing that I'm right behind her.

My head is on a swivel as the two of us drive through her neighborhood. *Stanfield Heights.* I don't know who the Stanfields are or why they have an entire community of McMansions named after them, but these places are shocking.

They each tower over the road, huge brick homes with

wraparound porches, large columns, and French doors on the second floor that lead out to additional porches. I can't help the zing of excitement that shoots through me as I drive by BMWs, a Lexus or two, and even matching Range Rovers in one driveway.

This is where I belong, not at the bar where I work, not in my dumpy apartment, not surrounded by people who only drink drip coffee that's a few hours old.

I belong here, with spray tans and nice cars, latte art, and Eliza.

When she turns to the right, I stop, then wait for her to pull into the garage before slowly driving by her house. I recognize it even though I've never been here before, all thanks to the posts she makes on Instagram and in her blog. How many times have I seen her front porch decked out for various holidays, with Penelope posed right in the middle of it all?

I grin to myself as I think about how Penelope dressed up as a cat last Halloween and posed with a jack-o-lantern she'd carved. Judging from how good it looked, the truth is that Eliza probably carved it for her, but who's counting? Everything in Eliza's life is perfect, and I want to be a part of it.

I gape at the flower beds in her front yard, all of them in full bloom and gorgeous, at the potted plants on the deck, at the deck furniture that looks straight out of a magazine.

And when I close my eyes, I can't help but see me sitting there on the porch with her, drinks in our hands, chatting as James grills out. Maybe he'll have a single friend he can introduce me to, and we can double-date. Penelope would be the cutest little flower girl at our wedding.

I know that I'm making a huge mistake pulling into Eliza's driveway, but I just can't help myself. It's like my car wants to be parked there in her driveway, right behind her garage door. Before I know what's happening, I'm getting out of the car, the sound of my door slamming shut loud in the quiet of the neighborhood.

My feet eat up the brick walkway to the front porch, and I hesitate there, not wanting to get any dirt on the clean welcome mat right outside the front door. My hands feel clammy, and for just a moment, I think about hurrying back to my car and driving away before anyone knows I'm here. But I refuse to give up on Eliza like that.

If she didn't want a friend like me, then she shouldn't have shared so much of her personal life online. All I'm doing is giving her the one thing I've noticed is missing in all of her posts.

11

ELIZA

"How was the coffee shop?" James greets me with a cautious smile when I walk into the kitchen, dumping my purse on the table and putting my phone carefully next to it. He's sitting where I left him, at the counter, his tablet in front of him opened to the news. I wonder for a moment where the kids are, then hear a soft thud from upstairs that lets me know the two of them are in their playroom.

"It was good. Different. A little nice to go somewhere I hadn't been before, but the latte didn't taste as great." I'm careful with what I say, mostly because I don't want to tell my husband the real reason I picked a new coffee shop this morning. I made the mistake of telling him I was going to be going somewhere new as I walked out the door, but the last thing I want to do is tell him why.

Bethany.

I don't know what the woman wants, and I don't want to think that she might be dangerous, but there was just something so unnerving about her showing up twice at places she knew I'd be, and then passing it off like it was some great coincidence. The last thing I want is for her to try to get closer to me and find out the truth about Knox.

"Glad to hear it. The weather is supposed to be pretty decent today, so I want to spend as much time working outside as possible before the storm moves in tomorrow. Thanks for making that happen for me with the kids."

I hear exactly what James is saying, and I also pick up on what he's not. He's not interested in helping out around the house today, which would normally be fine, but I had a photo shoot planned for True Green, and the last thing I want is to have the kids running around while I'm doing that.

Them getting in the way or distracting me is when I'd get sloppy, when my pictures wouldn't look the way I really need them to. Instead of arguing with him, though, which I'm sure won't work out in my favor, I force a smile to my lips and nod. "Whatever you need, James. You're so supportive of the work I do that I want to make sure I'm there for you."

I don't miss the surprise that flits across his face, but before he can respond, the doorbell rings, and we both freeze.

This is it.

This is the one thing that I've been waiting for since we took Knox from my sister's. It was the right thing to do, and I'll argue that until the day I die, but there's always been this small voice in the back of my brain telling me that it was going to come back and bite me in the ass eventually.

When I close my eyes, I can picture police officers standing out there, handcuffs at the ready, grim expressions on their faces. I highly doubt that they'll want to hear from me how we were saving my nephew, how much better his life is now that he has a family who loves him, how I'll do anything to keep him safe.

"Eliza." James' voice is harsh. "Are you going to get it, or do you want me to?"

The doorbell rings again.

Upstairs, the sound of Penelope and Knox playing has stopped, but I know my kids. I know how curious they are. I need to get to that door before they decide they should open it. Sure, we've warned Penelope against doing just that time and time again, but she's still a little kid, and little kids make mistakes.

I move quickly, my feet no longer feeling stuck to the floor as I race into the foyer and grab the lock, throwing it so I can open the door. James is behind me, and I hear feet pounding down the stairs.

"Get them upstairs," I hiss at James and then wait until he hurries away from me.

Making sure I'm smiling as big as I possibly can, I open the door, planting my foot behind it when I have it swung open enough to see outside, so that whoever is on the porch won't be able to force their way in past me. There's no way I'm letting the police in here without a warrant. They'd better have some really good reason to come knocking on my door right now and scaring me half to death.

I'm going to make sure they can't see Knox from the porch.

But it's not the police standing on my welcome mat. My mouth drops open slightly when I see who it is; then I feel a flush of anger heat my chest, making me feel like I've got a sunburn.

"Bethany?" Her name is foreign and dirty in my mouth; I spit it at her in shock. "What in the world are you doing here?"

And how did you find me? That's the question I can't ask, but I honestly feel like it's hanging in the air between us.

"Hey, Eliza!" Bethany looks tired. I see the lines under her eyes, the dark spots that are showing through her concealer. She looks like she made an effort to keep from coming across exhausted, but she's definitely not as put-together as I am. "I noticed you didn't go to your usual coffee shop this morning, and I wanted to make sure you're okay."

My head spins as I try to work through what she just said. "You were watching me?"

Her eyes widen, and she actually takes a small step back, holding her hands up between the two of us. "Oh, no, nothing like that! I just thought I would join you for coffee this morning, and I was there early, so I bought your latte, then you didn't come, and I wanted to make sure you were okay."

There's a huge smile on her face, but it falters when I don't immediately answer.

I don't know what to say to this woman. Honestly, I'm horrified that she's standing here on my porch like I should be really happy to see her, when all I want to do is slam the door in her face and retreat into my house to gather my family around me. Nervously, I glance behind me at the staircase that leads up to the second floor, but there aren't any little faces there watching to see what's going on.

Thank God I sent James up there to keep Knox away from the door. The last thing I need is someone like Bethany, who seems a little too eager to be my friend, to see him.

"I'm fine." My voice is tight, even to my ears, but if Bethany can tell that I'm not happy to see her, she doesn't react. "Listen, I don't love the fact that you just showed up here at my house, okay? That's something only good friends should do."

She opens her mouth to argue, but I forge ahead, not wanting to give her the opportunity to speak. Bethany seems like the kind of person who will do whatever it takes to twist things around so that she can make herself look like she didn't do anything wrong.

"I don't know why you're really here, but whatever it is you want, you need to stop. Do you understand?"

Her cheeks are bright red, and I think I see the sparkle of angry tears in her eyes, but she doesn't reach up to wipe them away. Instead, her hands clench into fists. Bethany takes a deep breath, like she's trying to calm herself down, then another.

"I noticed you don't have any close friends," she says, her words slow, carefully chosen. "I thought that you might want one. I thought the two of us could be friends."

I stare at her, taking in her ill-fitting clothes, her limp hair, her cheap makeup. She's not a person I would ever want to be friends with, and it takes all of my self-control not to laugh right in her face. There's no way in hell the two of us would ever be friends. We're too different, our lives so far separated from each other's that it's insane to think we could ever bridge that gap.

Not that I'd ever want to. Even if Bethany hadn't totally creeped me out by showing up here at my house without an invitation, it's not like the two of us are anything alike.

Besides, how would she look in a selfie with me? Not great. I can only imagine what my Instagram followers would think if she ever appeared in my feed, and I don't want to risk losing any brand support by having her appear in posts on my blog. I've done everything I can to carefully curate my aesthetic. I'm not going to ruin it by having Bethany in photos.

"I don't need close friends," I say, speaking slowly and staring at her to make sure she's paying attention to what I'm saying. "I have my family; I have my job; I have my followers. I don't want a close friend who thinks it's okay to just show up at my house."

"Everyone needs friends," she begins, but I cut her off.

"No, Bethany. You need to stop. Whatever this is," I say,

waving my hand around between the two of us, "isn't really a thing. I don't want you showing up here. Forget where I live, do you understand me? Don't come here again, don't try to push me to be your friend. I don't want a friend, *Bethany*."

There. That should do it. Unless she's more obtuse than I thought at first, there's no way she could possibly misconstrue what I just said to her and how clear I was about it. When she doesn't respond, I give her a small nod, then back into my house, locking the door as soon as I shut it in her face.

She has to get the hint. I have a very good feeling that after this I won't hear anything from Bethany again for a long time, and the relief that runs through me makes me sag against the door.

I don't want friends, don't need friends, and certainly can't risk someone getting close enough to me to find out the truth. Bethany's a little pushy, but that's all, I'm sure of it.

12

BETHANY

I hate to think about how long I stood on Eliza's porch after she shut the door on me this morning. My face burns with the memory of how angry and twisted her face had looked, at how worried I was that her neighbors might be watching me through their windows, at the way she seemed to spit my name at me.

Now, standing in the back room of the Tipsy Cat, I tap on my phone, wanting to see if maybe she changed her mind. It's entirely possible that she went inside her house after getting so angry with me and realized how rude she was. I love the thought of her feeling terrible for treating me as badly as she did and apologizing.

I don't have any Instagram notifications, but I'm still going to log in and check to make sure she didn't send me a message or anything.

Nothing.

Gritting my teeth together, I tap the screen harder than necessary, navigating over to her profile.

But it's gone.

"What the hell?" I double-check the name I have typed in,

to make sure I didn't make a typo, but it's correct. Her profile is gone.

But I know she wouldn't have deleted it, not when she was making such a big deal this morning about having her followers and not needing friends. I log out of Instagram and then log back in, hoping that it was some sort of glitch and I can do a hard reset to make her profile appear.

But it's still gone.

Cindy walks into the back where I'm standing and leans past me to grab her bottle of water, unscrewing the top and taking a huge sip before I realize I can ask her for help.

"I need your phone," I say to her, slipping mine into my pocket and holding out my hand. My phone must be broken or something, but nothing really makes sense. Why wouldn't I be able to see her profile?

"Why?" She takes another sip, then caps the bottle, wiping the back of her hand across her mouth. I cringe at the thought of her waiting tables and handing out drinks like that but don't say anything.

"I think something's wrong with my Instagram account. I need to see if someone has posted."

"That mommy blogger you're in love with?" She grins at me. Even though I feel my stomach twist at her words, I somehow keep a smile on my face and don't snap back at her. "Oh, fine." She sighs. "But make it fast. I need to get some drinks out to a group of doctors, and they're being real pills."

My fingers feel fat, and I fumble her phone when I take it from her, but a moment later, I'm on her Instagram account. Navigating over to where I can search for a user, I carefully type in Eliza's handle. *PerfectCozyMom.*

It pops right up.

"What the hell?" I mutter the words, and Cindy scoots next to me, looking over my shoulder. "Why wouldn't I be able to see her account from my profile?"

"She must have you blocked," Cindy says, tapping the screen to open up Eliza's most recent post. I glance at her, a frown on my face, and she continues, "When you block someone, it's like your account gets completely deleted, not that it just goes private. You won't be able to see anything that she's done, and it's like they just disappear."

I hear the words she's saying, but I'm still staring at the picture enlarged on the screen. Something about it isn't right, but I can't quite put my finger on what it is.

Cindy takes her phone back from me, and I give my head a little shake, feeling like I'm waking up from a trance. "So you really think she blocked me?" It feels horrible to say those words, horrible to think that Eliza would do something like that to me when I'm just trying to be the friend she needs.

"You can't see her profile at all?" When I nod, Cindy shrugs. "Yeah, that's what she did. You're blocked. What the hell did you do to make a mommy blogger mad at you?"

I don't want to tell her that I showed up unannounced at Eliza's house. Judging by the way Eliza reacted, it really wasn't the right thing to do, but it felt right at the time.

"Hey, can you take a screenshot of that post and text it to me?" I lean forward, wanting to get another glance at the screen before Cindy turns her phone off.

"What in the world? You are in love with her, you know that?" Cindy peers at me, but I relax a little when she takes a screenshot and starts typing on her phone. "Are you gay or something? Not that I care, it's just that you're obsessed."

I shake my head. "No, I just..." How in the world could I ever tell Cindy how I feel about Eliza? It's not that I'm in love with her, not at all, but we really belong together. As friends. She needs me, and I need her. I want to be friends with someone as well liked as she is, want to know what it's like to have people really want to be around me, and she needs

someone like me to give her the support and love that
nobody else seems to.

"Whatever, like I said, I don't care. My brother is gay, so
I'm cool with it if you are. But you're going to have to get over
her. Isn't she married?"

I nod. My phone vibrates in my pocket, and while I want
to pull it out and stare at the picture Cindy just sent over to
me, I somehow manage to keep from pulling it out and
tapping on the screen.

"Cool. Well, I'm here if you need to talk, okay? But not
right now, because I need to get those drinks out if I'm going
to get a decent tip. You'd think doctors would tip better than
they do, but it's like their God complexes get in the way or
something. They're too busy thinking about how awesome it
was saving someone's life on the operating table to realize
that I need to make rent."

She brushes past me and walks back into the bar, her
head high, her shoulders back, doing whatever she can with
her body to make sure that not only will the doctors notice
her, but that they'll give her a good tip.

I should do the same thing. I know I have tables waiting
on me, and that if my boss finds me back here on my phone
instead of working my tail off, he's going to get mad at me,
and I might even risk losing my job. But now that Cindy's
gone, I really need to look at the screenshot she just sent me.

I can't put my finger on what it was, but there was something wrong in the picture Eliza posted.

Something I might be able to use against her. Leverage,
let's say.

Something that might make her change her mind about
being my friend.

13

ELIZA

I'm buzzing with excitement while I make lunch.

Having brands reach out to me is validating; it shows me that I'm more than a doctor's wife, more than just a mom. James is worried about Knox, but I'm careful, and I feel like I'm finally reaching a turning point in my work.

Companies starting to reach out to me could be huge for our family. No, it's not like we want for anything, and James and I don't have to budget, thanks to how much money he has from his parents and how much he makes each month, but as a wife who stays home with the kids, it can be frustrating to feel like you are only spending your husband's money.

James doesn't get that. I don't think he ever will, no matter how many times I try to explain it to him. So even though I know he'd love for there to be some changes around the house, I'm not changing anything. This is the way our lives are going to be for a while, and as I start to make more and more money, he'll see that I'm doing the right thing.

I wish he could be supportive just because he saw that my blogging made me happy, but that's not enough for him. I wish I could say I'm okay with that, but I'm not. I'll just keep working hard to make more and more brands want to work with me, and then I'll show him that what I do is just as valuable as what he does.

These are the thoughts running through my mind as I cut the crusts off Penelope's and Knox's PB&J sandwiches and then pile some chips on each plate. I picked up Cuties at the store over the weekend, knowing full well that they both love the little citrus fruits, and after I peel each of them a Cutie, I call them to the kitchen table.

Penelope runs in and sits right down, pulling her napkin onto her lap before grabbing a chip and popping it in her mouth.

"Where's your brother?" It's not like Knox to not be right on Penelope's heels. He loves to go wherever she does, so I'm a little surprised that she made it into the kitchen first without him chasing right behind her.

"Upstairs. Still playing with blocks." She shrugs and pops a segment of fruit into her mouth. "I can get him if you want."

"No, I'll get him." I'm hungry and need to work on a post for my blog, but if I don't get Knox down here to eat, then he's going to get hangry and fall apart right when I'm the middle of typing. Leaving my little girl at the table, I hurry upstairs.

"Knox?" Turning into the playroom, I call out for him. "Honey, it's time to eat." Penelope said he was playing with blocks, but he's not in the corner adding more blocks to the top of the tower the two of them have been working on all morning.

Sighing, I reach back and tighten my ponytail. I'm not in the mood to play hide-and-seek with him, especially since he's great at contorting his body to fit in tiny little spaces where I wouldn't normally think to look for him.

"Knox, honey? Come on out and get some lunch. There

will be ice cream when you finish your sandwich, and you can put the sprinkles on yourself." It's daring of me to say that, knowing full well that there will probably be more sprinkles than ice cream in the bowl, but I really want him to come on out and stop this little game.

Nothing.

Frustration bubbles up in me, and I close my eyes, taking a deep breath and counting to ten. Penelope is such an easy child and has always been like that. She's never been difficult, never once hidden from me like this, never pushed my buttons. She loves being in front of the camera—most of the time—and even when she doesn't, she'll put on the clothes I ask her to wear and slap a smile on her face so she looks the best she can.

Knox, on the other hand, loves to push every button he can, even though he's still so little. I attribute it to him being Camilla's son. She was the same way, but I'm his mother now, and I love him.

I'm not going to get angry at him for how Camilla raised him, and when I open my eyes, I feel calmer.

"Someone is going to eat all of the ice cream in the house if you're not careful," I say, my voice a singsong as I poke around the playroom. He's not hiding behind the sofa, not tucked next to the bookcase that's groaning with picture books. I check in the fort James made them over the weekend, but he's not there, either.

Maybe he's in his bedroom. I highly doubt that he would have put himself to bed alone, especially because he can be a bit of a nightmare about taking naps, but it's worth checking to see if he passed out on the rug in his room or anything. Peeking in his room, I feel my heart drop a bit when he's not there.

Where is he?

I don't like the way panic is bubbling up in me right now.

Even though I know there's no way he could have gotten out of the house without me knowing about it, fear eats at the back of my mind.

What if someone has seen him through a window?

What if he got hurt?

What if he's hiding from me on purpose because he suddenly hates me?

Bending over, I grab my thighs and force myself to breathe through my nose. Every once in a while Knox will hide from me like this, and while I always find him in the end, it still makes me feel sick to my stomach the entire time he's missing.

It's only when I'm this quiet that I hear laughter and little feet running past the door.

"Knox!" Standing, I cry out his name, happiness pushing away the fear that was taking over. "Baby, be careful on the stairs! Let me help you."

The doorbell rings.

"No," I whisper, racing from his room. "Knox, no, get away from the stairs! Come back to me!"

He doesn't answer, although it's not like I expected him to. By the time I reach the stairs, the unthinkable has happened.

Penelope knows not to go to the door and open it without a parent there with her. How many times have both James and I told her over and over that it's just not safe, that doing so could put her in danger, that she never knows who is trying to get in.

And Knox knows that when I call him, he's supposed to come back to me. He's supposed to turn and run to me, no matter what he's doing.

But I see Penelope unlock the door, and Knox is halfway down the stairs, his chubby hand gripping the handrail, his little feet moving as fast as they can go without making him pitch down the rest of the way.

"Penelope, no!" I cry out the words, reaching for my daughter like I'm going to be able to touch her from way up here on the second floor, like I'm actually going to be able to stop what's happening. Maybe I should be running down the stairs, should try to grab Knox up so I can hide him behind me, should try to do whatever it takes to stop her from opening the door and him from being seen, but I'm frozen in place, and all I can do is let my jaw drop open as Penelope swings the door wide.

Or does someone push it from the outside?

Does it matter?

Penelope stumbles back from the door. I'm still on the staircase, which leads straight down to the front door. I now have the perfect view of who is standing there on my welcome mat, who had the gall to come up and ring the bell, who my daughter let into the house.

Even worse...

They have a perfect view of me.

And of Knox.

14

BETHANY

I knew it.

I knew it from the moment I had Cindy take a screenshot of Eliza's Instagram post that something was going on in this house, that Eliza had a secret so big she was willing to do whatever it took to keep it hidden.

And so I drove over here this morning, practically vibrating with excitement, unable to control myself.

It's Monday, and from following Eliza's Instagram and blog, I know that she likes to spend all day Monday at home with Penelope.

With her kid.

Only it's not one, is it? It's two.

Kids.

Even though it almost killed me to wait this long, I knew I needed to make sure James would be at work, that he wouldn't accidentally answer the door, that he wouldn't be able to help his wife keep lying, the way he'd done for so long. And so, even though it drove me crazy, even though I couldn't sleep, I waited.

Until right now.

"I knew it," I breathe out, and Penelope takes a step back like she's afraid of me, but it's not her I'm staring at right now, it's the little boy taking each step one at a time as he works his way down from the second floor. His face is scrunched up in concentration, and behind him, still hovering at the top of the stairs like she's not sure what she should do, is Eliza.

Unlike the little boy, though, who isn't looking at me as he picks his way down the stairs, Eliza's staring right at me, hatred and anger mingled together on her beautiful face.

I know I should speak to Penelope, should thank her for opening the door, but all I can do is push past her and shut the door behind me. It smells delicious in here, and I let my eyes flick around the foyer, taking in the expensive art on the wall I didn't notice the first time, the wide wood planks on the floor, the cream-colored runner up the stairs.

It's like I just walked into a magazine.

"Knox, be careful!" Eliza's voice breaks me from my spell, and I look up right as the little boy teeters for a moment on the stairs, finally righting himself just as Eliza reaches him. She scoops him up, holding him against her chest, his head over her shoulder, then stalks to me. "What are you doing here? I told you I didn't want you coming around here again."

Her words drip venom, but the hand she reaches out to lightly take Penelope by the shoulder and pull her away from me is soft, gentle.

"I saw your post," I say, and suddenly all of the words I want to tell her dry up in my mouth. I'd planned what I was going to say to her my entire drive over here, but now that I see her face-to-face, now that I'm sure I was right about what I thought, it's like I can't get my tongue to form any of the words correctly.

Her eyes narrow. "I blocked you."

Even though Cindy had told me that and I'd suspected that my co-worker was right, it still hurts to hear Eliza say that. I gasp, my hand fluttering up to my chest. "But why? I told you we could be friends."

"And I told you I didn't want any." She pauses, then puts the little boy down on the floor before taking Penelope by the chin and tilting her daughter's face up to hers. "Go on into the kitchen and finish your meal, okay? I'll be in momentarily. I just need to say goodbye to this woman."

The nervous look Penelope gives me should make me feel bad about scaring her, but I'm honestly much too interested in talking to her mom to really pay attention to the little girl. I watch as she takes the boy by the hand and pulls him away from Eliza. For a moment, I don't think he's going to let go of Eliza's leg, but then he does, and they disappear, leaving the two of us alone.

It feels like all the air has been sucked out of the room. I should speak, should explain what's going on, but I can't seem to talk. This is the first time I've actually been inside Eliza's house, and while it's not going exactly the way I thought it would, it's still incredible to be here.

"I'm calling the police if you don't leave." Eliza pulls her phone from her pocket, but I notice that her hand trembles. "Go, Bethany, and don't ever come back."

"I knew you had a little boy here," I say, finally managing to speak. "But why are you hiding him?"

The look she gives me is sharp. "I'm not hiding him. You haven't discovered anything, Bethany. Go."

Her words are angry, but she doesn't slide on her screen and dial 911. She obviously wants to try to scare me off without actually going through with her threat.

But why?

"But I saw something," I say, ignoring the dark look on her face and the threat of the phone in her hand. "You slipped up, Eliza, you made it so I could tell that you had a little boy here, someone you've kept hidden for a very long time. You need to tell me who he is and why you don't want anyone to know that you have him."

I'm talking faster than I can think, but I really need her to know that I'm onto her. The last thing I want is for her to realize that I'm not willing to get involved with the police and push it with them. If she were to call...

Well, would I leave? Or would I stay here with her, waiting to let them know that she has a little boy in her house that I don't think she's supposed to have?

"You never released a birth announcement for him," I say, pointing in the direction the kids went. Eliza's eyes flick to the side, like she's trying to tell if I can see Penelope and the little boy from here, but I can't. I'm just proving my point, proving that I know a hell of a lot more about Eliza than she might want me to.

"Not everyone does all the time, especially for the second child." She lifts her chin.

"Bullshit." It feels good to swear, to see the look of surprise on her face. "You went over the top when Penelope was born, and judging by how old that little boy looks, you should have been posting about him on your mommy blog and Instagram. Why aren't there any posts about helping an older child deal with the stress and pressure of a new baby?"

"Because there wasn't any stress or pressure."

I shake my head. "Wrong. Because there wasn't any baby. There wasn't any pregnancy, and then there was. You think that I don't know this about you, Eliza? I told you—the two of us are going to be great friends. There's no reason to fight it, not when you and I are so much alike, not when you and I can be amazing friends."

I pause, wanting to see if she's going to respond, but her lips are pressed tightly together, like she's doing everything she can to keep from screaming at me. Her eyes are narrowed, her fingers still gripping the phone so hard the skin around her nails is turning white.

"Where did you get the little boy, Eliza?"

"Why are you here?" She snaps the question at me like my words suddenly broke her free from a spell she'd been under. "Really, Bethany, why did you come here, why are you on my porch, why are you throwing such ridiculous accusations at me?" She pauses, breathing heavily, and we're so much alike that I can actually fill in the silence, fill in what she wanted to ask but didn't.

How did you know the truth?

"I know you're hiding something about that little boy," I say, wanting to change the subject, needing to make her see what I see.

"You know nothing. Quit acting like you do." She cuts me off, and even though I need to tell her just how much that hurt to find out that she'd done that to me, that's something that we can talk about at a later time. Right now, we just need to get through this little rough patch, but we will.

Friends always do.

"Your last post had something in it. Here, let me show you." I fumble my phone as I turn it on and tap over to my saved pictures. I'm not nervous about what she might say when she sees the proof, just so excited to finally be here, finally be having this conversation, that I have to be careful not to drop my phone. "Okay, look."

Keeping my fingers tight around the phone so she can't pull it from me and then throw it or break it, I turn the screen towards Eliza, watching her face as she looks at the picture.

"That's my post, but all it does is show that you're creepy, that you somehow managed to look at my Instagram, even though I clearly didn't want you to. It proves nothing, and now I'm calling—"

"Look in the top right corner." Even though I know I

should try to remain calm, I can't help the smile that lifts the corners of my lips.

Eliza leans forward. I can smell the peppermint on her breath, feel her breath on my skin, she's so close to my phone. She squints, and I think for a moment that maybe I'm wrong, that I might have made a mistake. Sweat trickles down my back, and I want to turn the phone around to look at the screen and verify that I'm showing her the right thing.

But I keep my eyes locked on Eliza's face, and it's when I'm about to pull the phone back from her that I see it.

She frowns, just a bit, a flood of concern washing over her.

She sees it.

I was right.

15

ELIZA

The last thing in the world I wanted was to invite Bethany into my house, to see her in my space, to watch as a soft sigh left her lips as she sank onto my sofa. I picked this sofa out myself after James and I had Penelope, and I love it. It's thick, plush, on dainty legs, with tufting in the back and custom throw pillows I had sewn to match.

I don't like Bethany in my space, certainly don't like the way she's now looking around, drinking it all in, an eager expression in her eyes when they finally land on me.

"It's so nice to be able to sit and talk with you," she says.

It hits me that this woman has to be totally delusional. Why else would she be sinking into my sofa like this, looking so at home? Why else would she have demanded to talk to me about what's in my Instagram post the moment she saw my face fall?

And what did I do? I let her in. I invited her into my house, and now, like a parasite, I'm not sure how I'm ever going to be able to get her to leave. I shouldn't have let her come in, I know that, but what choice did I have? I told her I would call the police, like I actually had some leverage, but the last thing I want is for someone to look into where Knox is really from.

And, knowing this woman, she'd be screaming the entire time about how he really isn't my son, how she can't find any proof of him belonging to me.

I hate her.

"You look stressed," she remarks. It's only then that I realize I'm gripping the arm of my chair so tightly that my knuckles are turning white.

I force myself to relax my grip and take a deep breath, inhaling and exhaling, then finally look at her.

"What do you want, Bethany?" From upstairs, I can hear the TV. Both Knox and Penelope were thrilled when I told them to go turn it on. They don't get to watch much TV, and I'm sure I wouldn't like what they chose, but right now, the only thing that matters to me is keeping them out of the way so I can deal with the woman sitting across from me.

"Oh, you know. I want to be your friend." She leans forward a little bit, resting her elbows on her thighs. "And I'd love a glass of water, if you don't mind. Ice, of course. With lemon, if you have it."

Is she serious? I think for a moment she's just pushing me to see how far I'm willing to go to keep this civil, but she doesn't move from her perch, and the smile doesn't slide off her face.

"Give me a minute," I mutter, rising and stalking past her to the kitchen. I don't want to leave her alone in my home, but I have to somehow figure out what I'm going to do about her. As long as she doesn't go upstairs to where the kids are playing, then I think things are going to be just fine.

As quickly as possible, I pour her some lemon water from the pitcher I keep in the refrigerator, then hand it to her and sit back down across from her.

Bethany takes a sip and sighs, then smacks her lips and

puts the glass on a coaster on the coffee table. "I have to know. Am I the only one who picked up on the problem in your Instagram post?" She sounds eager, and I close my eyes for a moment, silently berating myself for ending up in this position.

Everything in my posts is curated, especially when it comes to Penelope. She's a little princess who loves fluffy dresses and skirts, pink and pearls, and never deigns to play with *boy toys*.

Ugh. I always hated that term, hated the thought that some parents made their kids feel like they could only play with pink girly toys if they were a girl, but as soon as I really started to take off online and gain more and more followers, I got sucked right into it. I clearly remember boxing up all the cars and blue trucks Penelope had, and then deleting any posts that showed them.

I needed her to look perfect, and I've always done a great job of doing that.

Until now.

"I am, aren't I?" Bethany claps her hands together in plea-sure and then kicks off her shoes, curling up into the corner of the sofa like she's getting comfortable enough for a movie. "You're so careful with your posts, you know that? I admire that. Everything looks... *just so*." Mockingly, she kisses the tips of her fingers like she's an Italian chef.

"So one post with a bit of a blue sippy cup in it made you think that I had a little boy in the house?" I'm almost afraid to ask the question, but I can't deny the fact that I really want to know what's going on in her head. She looks a mess at first glance, but there's obviously something more to her than I thought.

Not that that's a good thing.

"The sippy cup inspired me to do my research," she says, taking another sip and then nodding like the water passes inspection. "I went online and just... dug deep, I guess you'd say. Went down the rabbit hole." She chuckles.

I don't.

"You stalked me."

"We're friends," she says with a shrug. "I was just learning about you. It has to be hard, being married to a man who is married to his job, and handling everything around the house on your own, but you never once missed out on an opportunity to share information about Penelope with the world. But that got me thinking... you share everything about your daughter, but what's going on with this sippy cup? Why isn't there a birth announcement, pictures of him on social media, no information from a few years ago about a baby shower?"

I grit my teeth. She wants me to fill in the gaps of what she's learned, but there's no way I'm going to help her out.

"Because you didn't actually give birth to him, did you?"

The accusation hangs heavy in the air between us. I know I shouldn't look to the stairs, shouldn't check on the kids, but I can't help but turn my head in that direction, relaxing a little bit when I hear the sound of their TV show.

"He's not yours, Eliza," she says. "No baby bump pictures, no maternity shots. So I went deeper, looking for any information about adoption that I could find. That stuff is iron-clad, by the way. No getting information there, but that just told me I needed to come here and talk to you face-to-face. Like friends."

"We're not friends."

"You think that now." She's getting frustrated, and I wonder if I made a mistake in pushing her away so hard. What she doesn't know is that James and I are both willing to do whatever it takes to protect Knox, to protect our family.

Because of that, I haven't called the police yet. I still feel like I can deal with this on my own.

"We may not be friends *now*," she says, changing tactics and taking a deep breath. "But friends do one thing that other people don't."

I don't want to ask her what she's talking about, but the question leaves my lips before I can stop it. "What's that? What do friends do?"

This makes her grin. If I were watching this on TV, then I'd know that this was the moment when the main character really messed up, when they lost the battle with another person, when everything in their life started to turn against them.

Only I'm not watching this, I can't turn it off, and the only thing I can do is feel the way my stomach sinks as she grins at me.

"They keep each other's secrets, Eliza. Now, tell me, do you want me to be your friend or not?"

16

BETHANY

That went a lot better than I originally thought it was going to. Eliza is so prickly, so unwilling to let people in. I sashay away from her front door, turning once at my car and waving back at her.

She's on the porch, arms crossed, a wary look on her face.

And honestly? I don't blame her.

It's so hard to let someone new in, to make a connection with a person you don't know very well, to let down your guard enough to make another person feel at home. We just took some major steps in our friendship, and I know that can be painful. It's so much easier on the heart to do this back-and-forth dance when getting to know someone.

But that's not what I want, and that's why I just ripped the Band-Aid off while we were talking.

We're going to be friends; I'm going to see to that. Eliza sees it now, too, sees that I know her secrets and that she needs to trust me. She has to see that I told her the truth about what I know not because I wanted to scare her or upset her, but because I want to be there for her.

I'm still not sure who the little boy is to her or where he came from, but I do know one thing.

His name is Knox.

And even better, I got to meet him.

It was thrilling to watch him and Penelope come down the stairs to meet me. I'd already met the girl before, of course, that one time at Target, but the little boy—Knox—was a stranger to me until just a few minutes ago.

Until I told Eliza that I was more than willing to call the cops and tell them she had some little boy living in her house that she wasn't supposed to.

For a moment, I thought she was going to call my bluff. Fear ran through me when I thought I'd made a mistake, that maybe he really is her son, but she didn't do anything of the sort.

I was right all along. Knox doesn't belong in that house, and now I'm going to find out who he really is. It's clear Eliza wants to keep him hidden away from people, but that's not any sort of life for a child. Luckily for him, he now has me in his life, an honorary aunt who will do whatever it takes to make sure he's happy.

And all because his mother and I are now best friends.

I'm whistling to myself as I pull into the public library parking lot. Sure, I have the internet on my phone, but it's hard to do any meaningful research online with a teeny tiny little screen, and I can use the computers here for free. This is where I came to dig into Eliza's past and look for any information about a baby shower she might have had for a little boy.

And this is where I'm going to find out who Knox really is.

Was it dangerous confronting Eliza without having all of my information and ducks in a row? Sure, she could have called the cops, thrown a fit, thrown me out.

But she didn't.

And that tells me that the truth is something she really wants to keep hidden.

I settle into a computer chair and rest my hands on the keyboard, wondering where exactly to start. I got a little information from Eliza just now, like the fact that she grew up in foster care and that she has a younger sister, but she didn't share much information about her besides her name.

Camilla.

I may not be the world's best internet sleuth, but I'm pretty sure that with this new information from Eliza, I can figure out exactly why she keeps Knox hidden, exactly why she didn't call the police when I showed up at her door.

"Okay, Camilla," I say, finally tapping away on the keyboard, "let's find out everything there is to know about you. I wouldn't be a very good friend if I didn't know all about Eliza's sister, would I?"

I'm not leaving here until I know the truth about Knox. Knowing that she has him isn't enough. There's more to it, I know there is, and I think it has to do with her sister.

I'm going to find out what it is, and then, when we share the same secret, she won't ever be able to deny my friendship.

17

ELIZA

"**M**ommy, are you okay?" Penelope grabs at my leg, wrapping her arms around it and pressing her face into my thigh as I stand at the kitchen counter, my hands flat on its surface, gulping in lungfuls of air. "Mommy?"

"I'm fine, darling," I say, patting the top of her head absentmindedly. "Mommy just really needs to talk to Daddy, and he's not picking up his phone or texting me back."

A shiver runs through me when I think about James at work, taking care of patients, talking with co-workers, completely unaware of what's going on at home. I have to fight the urge to throw the kids in the car and drive to see him so I can talk to him in person.

How would I explain Knox to anyone who asked if I took him to see James at work? I'd have to tell them that I was babysitting him, that he wasn't mine, but then if he called me *Mommy* in front of anyone...

"I need a snack," Penelope whines.

Even though I doubt she's hungry, I shoo her back upstairs with her brother while I put together a plate of crackers, cheese, and fruit. It feels good to have my hands busy while I wait on James, but every time I look at my silent phone on the counter and it doesn't ring, I feel my blood pressure going up.

"Come on," I mutter, stopping to check it to make sure I didn't miss a text from him.

Nothing.

My phone sits silent, and I grab it, shoving it into my pocket before taking the plate of food up to my kids. They're both sitting way too close to the TV, watching some mind-numbing show about talking baby dinosaurs, but I don't have the energy right now to correct them.

I need to talk to James.

It's only when I'm pacing in the kitchen, about ready to come out of my skin, that the phone rings. I fumble it from my pocket, afraid for just a moment that it's going to be Bethany, but I relax when I see James' name on the screen.

"James, she came here," I gasp out, sinking onto a stool at our breakfast bar.

"Who did?" He's confused, and I close my eyes, taking a deep breath so I don't get frustrated with him. It's not his fault that he's not here living this hell with me. Of course he wouldn't know right away what was going on.

"Bethany. That woman I told you about who keeps showing up places. She came here." I glance around the room to make sure the kids haven't snuck silently down the stairs. "She knew about Knox."

James is silent for so long that I pull the phone away from my ear and check it to make sure I haven't lost him.

"James?"

"I'm here." Another pause. I hear voices behind him, and I wonder if he's standing outside on the sidewalk or in the break room. "How did she know?"

This is the part I don't want to admit to my husband, but

as much as I'd like to hide it, I know I need to come clean. "She saw one of his sippy cups in a post I made on Instagram."

"Eliza—"

"It was an accident!"

"But now someone knows." His voice is harsh. When he speaks again, it's a little softer, and I wonder if that's because he realized how he was talking to me, or because someone is listening to him. "This could ruin everything. This could ruin *us*."

"I know; you think I don't know? I screwed up, is that what you want me to say?" Sweat breaks out on my brow, and I wipe my hand across my forehead. "I screwed up, okay? I admit it. I've always been so careful. I don't know how she was paying that close attention. And I blocked her, so someone must have shown her, or she made a new account or..." My voice trails off.

"What did she want? Did she call the police?"

I shake my head, then remember he can't see me. "No, nothing like that. I mean, she would. She's evil, but she doesn't want to turn us in. She wanted to know who he was." I swallow hard, not wanting to admit this last part to my husband. It's too crazy to even say. "And she wants me to be her friend."

"What?"

"Her friend. She wants the two of us to be good friends, to spend time together, to hang out. She wants to come over for dinner and go shopping together, and for me to pretend like she doesn't know this crazy secret of mine and is lording it over me!"

"You need to calm down." He's maddening right now, and I bite down hard on my knuckles to keep from screaming at him. "What did you say to her?"

"At first I told her she was crazy, but what choice do I

have, James? She really wants to be friends, and she knows about Knox."

"What did you tell her about him?"

Closing my eyes, I picture the scene. Bethany kept pushing, wanting me to be honest with her about where Knox came from and who he was. When I wouldn't answer, she switched up the topic of conversation, asking instead about my childhood and family. Those questions were easier to answer, so I did.

Even when she asked about a sister. I told her Camilla's name. I probably shouldn't have, but she just kept pushing and pushing. I felt like I was going to go insane if she didn't stop asking me questions, and I finally slipped, my sister's name falling from my lips before I could stop it.

It's been years since I mentioned her to anyone besides James.

But I don't think I should have done that. My stomach turns, and I push the fear that Bethany will find out the truth about Camilla away.

"I told her he was ours, but that we didn't want to put him in the public eye until he was old enough to make that decision the way Penelope had." It was a good lie. It would work.

"And she bought it?"

"I think so. She left, telling me she had some errands to run, but she made me give her my phone number, and told me she'd be in touch."

"Eliza, you need to fix this. I can't leave work. I can't take care of this for you. Do you even know what she's capable of? What she really wants? For her to say she wants to be friends with you... that's not normal. She's not sane."

"I know she's not," I hiss. "You think I don't know that? I'm going to do whatever it takes to get her out of my life. I'm certainly not ever going to let her know the truth."

"I told you the blogging—"

I cut him off. "The last thing I need is to hear that from you right now," I tell him. My head pounds, and I get up, walking to the junk drawer by the sink to look for some painkillers. "I'm going to fix this. You have to trust me. Just let me think through what I'm going to do next."

"We'll lose it all," James tells me, like I don't already know that. Like I'm not totally aware of the threat this woman poses to my family and all of the things James and I have worked so hard to build together.

"Let me think it through," I snap; then I hang up on James before shaking out a few pills and swallowing them without water. Hanging up on my husband isn't going to solve anything, but neither is listening to him chatter on and on about what I need to do.

I have to take care of Bethany, and while the last thing I want to do is let her into my life, that might just be the thing I need to do.

Maybe, instead of pushing her away, I need to get closer to her.

It might be the only way to stop her from being a threat.

18

BETHANY

I wake up the next morning to a text on my phone from Eliza. Rolling over, I rub the sleep out of my eyes and squint at my phone's screen while I try to make out the words.

Do you want to go shopping this evening?

Tuesday isn't Eliza's normal day to go shopping. From what I've gathered, she likes to spend Tuesday evening at home with James and the kids, so for her to reach out to me and invite me out means just one thing.

She's decided that she wants to be friends with me.

I'm exhausted from a long shift serving drinks and dealing with unruly customers, but that doesn't stop me from sitting up and texting her back right away.

I'd love to. I'll pick you up at 6. xx

There. She doesn't know where I live yet, and while I'd love for her to drive me around so I could enjoy her nice car,

I'm not sure if I'm ready to tell her where I live. My apartment isn't nearly as nice as her house is, but I'm sure that, given time and her getting to really know me better, she won't mind.

Given enough time, she's just going to be so happy to have me in her life that she won't care one bit what my place looks like, and then I hope to move in with her.

Let's meet at Target. 6:30

"Come on," I mutter, but instead of arguing with her, I toss my phone onto my bed and stretch, getting up to take a shower. It's frustrating that she wants to take control and not let me make the plans, but I have to remind myself that she's new to having friends. I know that when a friend offers something, you accept.

But I'm Eliza's first friend. She'll learn how to be a better one eventually. It will just take some time.

Before, I might have been worried that she would want to cancel on me or change our plans, but I know that's not going to happen, and that's because of what I found out at the library yesterday. Eliza made a huge mistake telling me her sister's name. I already knew Eliza was raised in Canada.

Camilla in Canada.

I wasn't able to find her, no social media, not like her sister Eliza, but I was able to find out something so interesting, I was willing to pay to print it off. Normally, I'll just take pictures of the computer screen with my phone if there's something I want to remember, so I don't have to pony up the cash to use the library's printer, but yesterday was special.

I think even the librarian was surprised when she saw me printing page after page, and then coming to her to pick it up and pay for it, but there was no way just taking pictures of the computer screen was going to ensure that I didn't miss a single detail.

Then, before I went to work last night, I sat on my bed here and read it over and over.

I know all the details.

Camilla is a druggie, a far cry from her sister, Eliza, but seems at first glance to just be another victim of a shoddy foster family. Maybe if the girls had had a better caseworker, then things would have turned out better for Camilla, but, as my mom used to say, you can wish in one hand and shit in the other and see which one fills up faster.

I couldn't find much else about the life Camilla had when she was younger, but it's not her sob story I was really interested in. No, the thing I was so willing to pay to print was a news article about a missing child, a little boy, apparently taken from her when she was passed out after a drug binge.

Eliza didn't mention this.

The police hadn't been entirely confident that she was telling them the truth about what happened to her son, that much was clear from the article, but Camilla, even though most people would call her a useless druggie, wasn't about to back down and ignore the fact that someone had taken her son.

From what I read, she raised hell. It's not that she sobered up very long, and it certainly didn't stick, but there were enough moments of lucidity for her to call the local papers, protest at the police department, and beg for a pro bono lawyer to bring her little boy back.

Of course, when the police went to the drug house where she'd been staying, all they found were used diapers and a few ratty pieces of toddler clothing.

Oh, and the needles and drugs in her room, which they promptly used as evidence to arrest her. She got out eventually, and from what I can tell, most people just thought she was a drug addict who dreamed up having a little boy.

If they only knew the truth.

So even though there were a few write-ups in the paper about her missing boy, and even though she swore up and down that she had a son, nobody had any proof that he existed.

But I think that I do.

Why else would Eliza be willing to hide a child away from the world? The only thing that makes any sense to me is that he isn't her son, and she isn't trying to protect her child.

She's trying to protect herself, because she kidnapped him from her sister.

I get it, I really do. I'm absolutely the last person to judge someone based on the decisions that they made in the past, especially if they believed they were doing the right thing for someone they loved. However, you can't just take a child, even from family, try to pass that child off as your own, and think that nobody is going to call you out on it.

Everyone has a skeleton in their closet, and I was willing to do whatever it took to find Eliza's so that I could use it to get her to spend time with me. I didn't think that it would be this big a skeleton, however, and I certainly didn't think I'd be able to find it this quickly.

It feels really, really good.

That's why, even though I'm not thrilled about having to wait so long to see Eliza today, I'm willing to be patient. She'll learn soon enough that I'm perfectly safe to have around her kids, that I won't do anything to hurt them. Tonight is the first time we're going to hang out together. I'm going to do whatever it takes to make it perfect.

BY THE TIME I need to leave the house for my Target date with Eliza, I'm so nervous I've changed my outfit three times and had to wash up with a washcloth so my pits don't sweat. I don't normally get nervous, not like this, but it's my first real friend date with Eliza, and I want it to go well. I lock up, even though it's not like I have anything valuable enough for someone to steal, then drive the ten minutes to Target, running over and over what I want to say to her in my mind.

Up until now, I've been perfectly confident. This is new territory for me, though. Sure, I've had friends before, but mostly women I work with, and that friendship always ends when we clock out at the end of our shift. Having someone I'm going to spend time with like this, outside of work, because we both really want to see each other, is new and different.

And thrilling.

Slowly driving through the parking lot, I search for Eliza's car, but so many of them look the same here. It's my car that really sticks out, but instead of parking it at the back of the lot and trying to hide it, I park right up front. This way, Eliza can walk me to my car when we're finished here.

She has no reason to be ashamed of me, and I'm going to make sure she's not.

Inside, I consider ordering a latte from Starbucks, but decide to wait. Eliza's the one with all the money, so she can pay for it; otherwise it's going to be a bit expensive for us to be friends. I'm sure she'll understand that I need her to pony up the money for me to have a coffee drink with her when she's the one with a husband making the big bucks.

6:20 comes and goes, and even though I know Eliza's not technically late, I can't help feeling nervous as I stare at the doors, waiting on my friend. They open and close, groups of laughing teenagers walking through, followed by harried-looking parents, even some single adults who are obviously on a mission as they hurry through the store.

But no Eliza.

It's 6:30. I'm nervous as I check my phone for any messages she may have left me, letting me know that something's going on. Surely she wouldn't cancel on our first date like this, would she? She knows how important it is to keep everyone in the dark about the little boy living in her house, and she also knows I'm the only person in the world who can help her do that.

So where is she?

I stalk back and forth between the checkout and cart return, growing more and more agitated.

6:35.

6:40.

"She did this to herself," I mutter, anger washing over me. "I didn't want to turn her in. I just wanted to be friends. I don't know why she wouldn't take me seriously."

Because I'm not looking where I'm going, I accidentally bump into an older woman walking by with a cart full of bags. She glares at me, and I apologize, muttering the words as I stare into the parking lot.

It's slowly getting dark out.

But Eliza still isn't here.

I'm going to make her pay for this.

"Shit. Shit, shit, shit. Shit!" Slamming my hands against the steering wheel feels really good, but doesn't do anything to change what just happened. Exhaling hard, I close my eyes and count to ten, a trick that has saved me more than once from overreacting with the kids, then get out of my car and walk around to the trunk to see how bad the damage is.

The person who rear-ended me is a teenager. I eyeball him, trying to decide if he's even old enough to be behind the wheel of a car. I'm a terrible judge when it comes to telling how old someone is, but he looks like he's twelve.

His glasses are askew, and he settles them back where they belong as he stares at where the front of his car has crumpled right into the back of mine. My right rear wheel is at a strange angle, and I have a sinking feeling the problem is a broken axle.

"I didn't see you stop," he says, and I glare at him, looking for the phone that I'm sure he was staring at when he plowed right into me.

"I'm sure the cops will love to talk to you about that," I

snap. I already called them, of course. They were the first phone call I made when he slammed into me, sending my head snapping forward and causing my seatbelt to tighten painfully across my chest. I'll probably have a bruise there, and I trace my fingers along my collarbone, wincing as I touch the already sensitive flesh.

"You didn't call the cops, did you?" He freezes in place and shakes his head. "Man, my parents are going to kill me."

"That's not my problem." I'm sure I should be kinder to him, should at least be asking him if he's hurt or needs me to call an ambulance, but I was already so stressed out before the accident that, quite frankly, I don't feel like I can spare him any sympathy.

This night is terrible. First I had to leave my family because I'm being blackmailed by a creepy woman I don't even know; then I get in an accident with the wonder kid who was obviously not paying attention to the road or to the fact that I was stopped at a red light.

James had offered to come pick me up, but he'd have to bring both kids with him, and this place is going to be crawling with cops. It would be stupid of us to bring Knox here when someone might pay attention to him. Not that any cop would really have a reason to look twice at a little boy who showed up with his dad, but still...

It's not worth it.

"Hey, do you know how long this is going to take? I was supposed to be home for dinner." The kid gets my attention, and I shake my head at him, my lips tight.

Then I realize what he just said, and I glance down at my watch, panic flowing through me.

It's 6:45. I'm late.

Really late.

My fingers feel numb as I look for Bethany's number in my phone, and even though I promised myself I wouldn't ever call the wretched woman, I find myself praying that she's going to pick up as I press my phone against my ear.

It rings once, twice, three times, and I'm terrified it might go to voicemail and Bethany will do something stupid, like tell someone that Knox isn't mine, when she picks up, ice in her voice.

"You're late."

"I know," I sputter, turning away from the accident and the teenager who can't seem to stop staring at me. "I was in an accident. Bethany, I'm so sorry, please don't do anything stupid. I was almost there, and this idiot rear-ended me at a red light."

"Hey!" the teenager shouts from behind me, but I ignore him. He's an idiot. An idiot staring at his phone instead of driving, and now I'm the one who has to try to fix his mistake.

Bethany's voice softens immediately, which is something I didn't expect to happen. "An accident, really? Are you okay?"

I nod, swallowing down the lump in my throat. It's been a long time since I was in a car accident, and I'd honestly forgotten just how scary they can be. "I'm okay," I say, "but my car is pretty messed up, and we're just waiting on the cops to get here."

As soon as I tell her that, I realize that I've made a huge mistake. This isn't James I'm talking to, not some mom I met who is going to be a supportive friend.

It's Bethany, the woman who stalked me and is obsessed with me for some reason.

"Where are you?" Even through the phone, her excitement is palpable. "I'll come to you, pick you up. I'll wait with you, and then I'll get you home in one piece. You don't have to go through this alone. We're friends."

I close my eyes and take a deep breath before I speak, hoping that will make me sound less stressed than I feel right now. "That's so kind of you, Bethany, but you don't need to do that. I've got it under control."

"Is James going to pick you up? With Penelope and Knox?"

How does she always stay one step ahead of me?

"No, but I can call a taxi or an Uber. It's no problem."

"Where are you? Because I'd love to tell you where I'm going right now."

Her tone of voice terrifies me, and I glance around, suspicious that she might already be here, might be watching me from one of the cars driving past. "Where are you going?"

"The police station."

A chill runs through me. "Don't. Bethany, don't do that." I cup my hand around my mouth so nobody else will be able to hear what I'm saying. "I didn't mean to miss our Target date, okay? I had an accident; it wasn't even my fault. Please don't do anything rash. We'll both regret it."

Silence. My heart beats so hard I feel like I'm going to throw up. Behind me, I hear the soft cry of sirens, and I know help is on its way, but before I can talk to an officer about what happened, I need to deal with Bethany. I have to get her to see that what she's doing is insane and will only backfire.

"Where are you, Eliza?"

Four simple words, but the threat is clear in her voice. I need to tell her where I am, and right now, or she's going to go to the police with whatever information she's found about Knox. The ball may be in my court, but Bethany is in total control. We both know it.

"The corner of Kanuga and King Street," I finally say. "Right by the old gas station. You can't miss us."

"See you soon," she chirps, the dark tone in her voice gone. "I'll be there in just a few minutes, and I'm going to take care of everything, I promise. You won't have to worry about a thing. I'm so glad you made the right choice. I wouldn't want anything bad to happen to you."

She hangs up, and I shiver, even though the air isn't cold. Talking to Bethany chills me, and I need to warm up, but it's hard with her words ringing in my ears.

I wouldn't want anything bad to happen to you.

From someone I considered a friend, I would love to hear that. I'd know they were looking out for me, that I could trust them, that they would be there if something terrible happened. It would be a promise of their love and support, no matter what I was going through.

But it doesn't sound like a promise from Bethany.

It sounds like a threat.

20

BETHANY

I see the police lights cutting through the growing dark before I reach the intersection where Eliza got into her car accident. She sounded fine on the phone, just a little shaken, and I'm so glad I can be here for her to make sure she's going to be safe. There's no reason for her to go through something this traumatic and scary on her own, not when I'm here to keep her company.

It's the right thing to do. It's something a friend would do, and I'm her friend now, so it makes sense she'd let me be here to help her out.

I park in the gas station parking lot and hurry over to where she's talking to an officer. He doesn't look when I walk up, and I loop my arm through Eliza's, pulling her close to comfort her.

She starts and acts like she's going to pull away from me, but I'm not letting her go. I'm here for her. I'm going to support her in every way possible.

The officer finally glances at me. "Sister?" he asks.

"Friend," I correct. "Sorry to interrupt your conversation. I got here as quickly as I could."

After giving me a brief nod, he continues. I listen to every word.

"I'm going to write him a ticket for distracted driving. He's at fault, so your insurance company will appreciate hearing that, as it will allow you to get repairs or money for your vehicle without too much of a problem. Now, it's not drivable, as I'm sure you can tell," he says, waving his hand to indicate her crunched vehicle, "but it looks like you're in good hands right now, so I'm going to finish up my paperwork and bring you copies of everything you're going to need."

"She's in great hands," I tell him. "Thank you for your help."

Eliza doesn't say anything as he walks away. Poor thing is probably in shock, and I'm really glad I'm here with her and that I didn't go to the police about Knox. Sure, I got a little upset there for a minute, thinking that she didn't want to be my friend any longer, but that was silly.

Of course she wants to be my friend. Something held her up, that's all, and I'm just really glad it wasn't anything worse than a simple fender bender.

"How are you?" I ask, turning to look at her. "Did you get hurt? What can I get you?"

She pulls her arm out of mine. Even though I don't want to let her go, I allow her to step back from me. It'll give her a chance to catch her breath, and will let me get a better look at her so I can make sure she's not hurt.

"I just want to go home," she says, shaking her head. "I'm okay, a little sore, but I just want to go home and rest up."

"We can't go home." The words spill from my lips before I realize I'm going to say them. Eliza glances up sharply at me, a question written all over her face. "I mean, we had a friend date planned. We were going to go shopping, spend some time together. I don't think we need to cancel all of our plans just because of this."

She stares at me like I've lost my mind. "Bethany," she says, and even though I can tell she's not happy with me, it sends a thrill through me to hear her say my name. "I was just in a car accident. We didn't have a friend date planned because we're not friends. I had to spend time with you to keep you from—"

"From telling the world who you are?" I lean closer, dropping my voice. "There's a cop right there. Think really hard about what you want to say. We're friends. Admit it."

Eliza stares at me. Her gaze is unblinking. How many times have I seen pictures of her staring right into the camera, taking perfect selfies where she's posed everything and made herself look like she has her life completely together?

Hundreds of times, that's how many. And she does, or mostly, but she has one big secret that I don't want to use against her. But I will if that's what it takes to get what I want.

"We're friends," she says, but her words are tight, and her teeth are gritted. I think about correcting how she's speaking to me and asking her to try to sound happier about the prospect of having me in her life, but before I can, the officer walks back over and hands Eliza a few sheets of paper.

"That's everything you're going to need to give to your insurance company," he says. "The wrecker will be here in a few minutes to tow your car, and you can deal with that in the morning. Until then, I'm glad you have a good friend here who will drive you around, because you're going to need someone taking you places."

"You really don't think they can fix it quickly?" Eliza locks eyes on the officer, worrying the papers in her hands. "I don't think I can handle not having a car."

"I'll drive you anywhere you need to go," I say, inserting myself in the conversation. The officer smiles at me, but Eliza doesn't look away from him. "Seriously, Eliza, you don't need to worry about a thing. I'm not going to leave you hanging, you know that."

She still doesn't look away from the officer. "Please," she says, "do you not think we can do something more tonight?"

He laughs. "Ma'am, I've done my part. Now it's up to your insurance company and up to his." He juts his thumb over his shoulder at the teenager. "The wrecker will come, take your vehicles, and you'll have to deal with this in the morning. If I were you, I'd get your friend here to drive you home, and be grateful that this wasn't your fault, you weren't seriously injured, and that you have someone so willing to help you out. More people should look for friends like you have."

He turns and walks away. I feel myself swell up with pride. I know that I'm a great friend and that Eliza and I are going to get along perfectly, but it feels really good to have the officer point it out.

"Do you want to go to Target and do some shopping, or is there somewhere else you want to go first?"

Eliza slowly turns, her eyes wide, and stares at me. I can't tell if she's excited about the prospect of us getting to spend so much time together this evening, or overwhelmed, but I'm here for her, no matter what she's feeling.

"I just want to go home," she says, enunciating each word like she thinks I'm having difficulty understanding her. "Please, Bethany, I just want to go home."

How disappointing. I make a show of turning and looking at the officer, who's currently talking to the teenager. The last thing I want to do is threaten Eliza again, but I need her to get it through her head that this night isn't over.

"Okay," she says, grabbing my arm and tugging on it a little so I'll turn and look at her. "How about this? I know we really wanted to hang out tonight, but my body is really sore. We'll go to your place and have a drink. Coffee, maybe?"

"You're that sore?" She nods, and I smile at her. "Okay,

then we don't have to go to Target, but I'm going to take you home so we can share a drink there, at your place. It's much nicer than mine, and besides, I'm sure James will want to see you to make sure you're okay, and I'd love to get to know your kids better."

She stiffens. "Target sounds fine," she suggests, but I shake my head, pulling my keys from my pocket.

"Nope, we'll get you home. You're right, Eliza, it was selfish of me to think that you'd have the energy to go shopping, but I'm sure you'll be happy at home. James can join us if he wants, of course, or it can just be some girl time. What do you say?"

I know what she's going to say even before she responds, and that's because Eliza isn't stupid. She's made some decisions in the past I don't necessarily agree with, and that could cause her problems if she didn't have someone like me looking out for her, but she's made it this far without anyone catching on to what she's doing.

That's why I know she's going to agree to let me take her home after the wrecker leaves. That's why I know she's not going to fight being my friend.

She has everything to lose, and I have everything to gain.

21

ELIZA

I see the surprise written all over my husband's face when Bethany and I walk into the house. He glances nervously at her and then pulls me into a hug, rubbing my back, murmuring in my ear.

Sinking into him, I try to let myself forget the terror that I felt when I was in that accident. Even though I walked away from it, I know it could have been so much worse, and then what would James have done? How in the world would he have managed being a single dad of two kids, one of whom doesn't really exist?

I'm sure if I voiced my concerns, Bethany would speak up and say she would be willing to help James, that she would do whatever it took to watch out for the kids and make sure they were taken care of while he was working. Honestly... the thought makes me sick.

Children need their mother. They need *me*. Something really bad could have happened to me when I was in that accident. I'm well aware of how lucky we all are that I'm safe, although a bit sore.

"Thanks for bringing Eliza home," James says to Bethany,

keeping his arm banded around my waist and turning to speak to the woman standing in our foyer. "I hate that I couldn't be there after her accident."

"I was so happy to do it," she says, a huge grin on her face. My night is ruined, but it honestly feels like Bethany couldn't be happier about the way things are going. "It was so scary when she told me what happened. I'm honestly just grateful she's okay and I could get to her so quickly, especially since you couldn't."

There's a barb there, and if I hoped that James wouldn't notice it, I'd be wrong. His fingers tighten on my waist, and he pulls me a bit closer, like he feels the need to claim me.

"Well, I appreciate you, and so does Eliza. Now, if you don't mind, I want to get her in some pajamas and make sure she's really okay." James is doing his best to get Bethany out the door, but I know it's not going to be this easy, and I'm right.

"She didn't tell you?" Bethany tilts her head like she's talking to a kid. "We were both so disappointed that we weren't able to get coffee and shop that we decided to hang out here for a little bit. I don't know if you want coffee or wine," she says, looking at me, "but I'll make it easy and have whatever you're having."

James pauses. I can feel the anxiety and confusion rolling off him in waves as he tries to figure out exactly what we're going to do. I was in the same boat as him on the way home, Bethany chattering up a storm the entire time she drove, me thinking hard about how I was going to get her to leave us alone.

"I think a glass of wine would be perfect," I say, shifting my weight away from my husband so I can look at him.

He looks surprised but nods, pulling away from me so he can get me something to drink. "Wine for you, then,

Bethany?" he asks over his shoulder, pausing before walking down the hall to the kitchen.

"Red, if you have it," she says, then turns to me, almost giddy. "Isn't this great? I really wanted to do some shopping with you and see if we could pick out some cute clothes together, but I think this is just as fun. Maybe even more so."

I watch in horror as she looks around the house, slowly walking down the hall away from me. We have family pictures on the walls, ones with just the three of us—not Knox—and she pauses at the first one, her head tilted to the side, a smile playing on her lips.

"No Knox?" Reaching out, she lightly taps the picture frame. I watch as it lists to the side. Without straightening it, she looks at me, waiting for my response.

"He wasn't here when we had that picture taken," I manage. I feel like I'm drowning, but I'm afraid to let her walk too far away from me, in case she were to find something I didn't want her to.

By the time James brings us the wine, we've made our way down the hall to the living room. I sit on the sofa, perched on the edge, unable to relax, the wine he handed me held in a tight grip. Bethany, though, kicks off her shoes and settles into the easy chair across from me, drawing her knees up to her chest and grinning at my husband when he hands her her wine.

"Thanks, James. Are you going to join us?" Her voice is light and unworried, like she doesn't have a care in the world.

I hate her.

"I'm actually going to go check on the kids," James tells her; then his eyes flick to me, like he's looking for support. I take a sip of my wine, then gulp some more, enjoying how it feels to have the alcohol warm my stomach. "I'll come check on you two in a bit."

He leaves the room. Neither of us make a move to stop

him. I hate Bethany being this close to my children, hate that she's in my house, hate that she obviously thinks she's coming out on top. The little grin on her face makes me want to punch her, and I have to take a deep breath and another sip of wine to control myself.

"Isn't this great? You have such a nice house, Eliza. I'm glad we could meet up here." Bethany turns from looking at the stairs to lock eyes on me. "You must love it here."

She obviously wants me to respond, and I nod, finally finding my voice. "I do. We do. It's a great house."

"I can see that. Is there a guest room?"

"What?" Her question takes me completely off guard. "A guest room?"

"Sure, for when you have family come to visit. Surely you have family come and stay with you once in a while."

Even though, on the surface, her words aren't threatening, I can't help the way my throat closes up a little bit at what she's saying. I feel like Bethany is playing with me, and I'm two steps behind, much too stupid to figure out how to handle what she's doing.

"I told you I have a sister," I begin.

She leans forward, clutching her wineglass around the stem, her eyes bright and locked on me. "You don't let your sister into this house, do you?"

What does she know? "We're not close, but she could stay here if she wanted to."

"Even with Knox?"

My heart hammers away in my chest. "What do you mean?" It's a silly question to ask, because if she knows enough to put two and two together with Knox and Camilla, then she knows the truth, and there isn't a damn thing I can do to pretend like she doesn't.

"Come on, Eliza, we're friends. Would you let Camilla come stay here with you, James, Penelope, and Knox?"

"If she wanted to." My mouth is dry, so I drink more wine.
"Even though she'd see her son?"

There it is. Any doubt I might have been clinging to that
Bethany didn't know the truth about what was really going
on in this house, about what had happened, flies out the
window. I should answer her, should try to argue with her or
tell her that she's got it all wrong, but all I can do is stare at
her, my mouth falling open, a strangled noise coming from
my throat.

"I. Know. Everything." She grins, and I feel my stomach
sink. "I don't want to threaten you, Eliza, because that's not
the type of friend I want to be, but you need to know that I
know the truth about you, about James, about Camilla and
Knox. It was all online. I found it all after you told me about
your sister. I won't tell anyone, of course. What you did
before we became friends isn't my business, but I know
about it."

"What do you want?" I'm staring at her, trying to make
this make sense, but I can't do it. Nothing makes sense, not
why she's here right now, why she's pushing this, what she
could possibly want to gain.

A flash of confusion crosses her face, and she laughs like I
just said the funniest thing she's ever heard. "Why, your
friendship, of course. You don't think it's anything more than
that, do you?"

"And you know about Knox?" I need to know for sure
where I stand with this woman, because right now I feel like
the ground has dropped out from underneath me. "You know,
and you're not interested in telling anyone?"

"I don't want to ruin your life, Eliza. That's what I need
you to understand." She's on her feet now, walking over to
me, the wineglass still clutched in her hand like she's trying
to choke it. "If I ruined your life, then I wouldn't get what I
want, would I?"

I don't want to know. I don't want to ask her the question I know I have to, but there isn't any choice.

I know it. She knows it.

Taking a deep breath, I ask the one question she's dying to answer.

22

ELIZA

Both of the kids are in bed, which is where James and I would like to be, too, but there's no way we can collapse into our king bed without figuring out what we're going to do about Bethany.

"What was the question she wanted you to ask her?" James looks exhausted, with dark circles under his eyes, but you'd never know it by how bright his voice is. We're both... not *excited*; that's not the word. But we're both running on pure adrenaline as we try to figure out what we're going to do.

"I asked her what she really wanted from me." My voice is flat to my ears. "I didn't think it would be that big a deal, to ask someone that. Hell, we ask the kids that all the time." Without thinking, I look straight up at the ceiling, imagining that I can see into their rooms, see them curled up in sleep.

They have no idea how scared I am of Bethany. It was one thing to think I had a follower who was just getting a little obsessed with me, but another to have her continually show up where I was and then demand this.

Undying friendship. Devotion.

"And she just wants to be friends?"

I nod. "That's what she said. Do I believe her? No, I don't think that I do, not when I can tell there's something more there that she really wants. It's not just friendship, James. The way she talks seems like she has this plan that I have no idea about, like she's already way ahead of me." I nibble on the cuticle of my finger. It's a terrible habit, and one I thought I broke a long time ago, but stress will cause you to do crazy things. As we sit in silence, my phone, which is on the coffee table between us, is constantly buzzing.

We're both used to that, but this time it feels ominous. Grabbing my phone, I swipe on the screen, then tap a few times to navigate to my Instagram profile. "Look," I say, handing James my phone.

"What is it?" I don't need to answer the question, because he can see for himself what I'm trying to show him. It's a picture of Bethany and me, one she demanded I take and post before she left. Our heads are together, like we're two great friends who want to be close for the picture.

The smile on her face is so huge it almost looks fake. I can tell just with a glance at my face that I don't mean my smile. It doesn't reach my eyes, and I look scared. Still, if you were to scroll by without really paying attention, I imagine you could miss the concern written all over my face.

"Who wrote the caption?" He glances up at me and hands me the phone. "'It's so nice to have a best friend I can trust with anything in my life.' Tell me that wasn't your idea."

"What do you think?" I snap the words at him and put my phone back on the coffee table, upside down so I don't have to look at the screen. "I didn't write that. She did. She wants me to be her best friend, James, but it's a sick game to her. We have nothing in common—nothing! But she doesn't care. She'll go to the police if I refuse her."

"Okay, hear me out." He leans forward, steepling his fingers together, which is how I imagine him talking to patients when things aren't great. "Do you think she'll move on from all of this and find someone else to latch onto? You're amazing, Eliza, you know that, but why in the world is she so obsessed with you? Why you?"

"I have no idea." Exhaling hard, I pull a blanket up to my neck and curl up under it. All I want is to go to bed and pretend none of this is happening, but there's no way to hide from what's going on in my life. "Seriously, I know what you're saying. I'm not that great, not to the point where someone should be this obsessed with me."

He sighs, and I feel my heart break. Never in my life did I mean for this to happen, for my blogging and social media to bring an absolute crazy out of the woodwork. I know he's doing his best to keep from saying *I told you so* after he asked me to give it all up.

I didn't, and now look where we are.

Of course, I know this is my fault, but how in the world was I to know that something like this would happen? Never in my wildest dreams did I think that someone as nutso as Bethany was out there watching my every move, reading my posts, checking my pictures to see where I was going.

And never in my wildest dreams did I think she'd be able to find out about Knox. That was something James and I went over time and time again, to make sure we didn't leave any clues behind that would let someone find out the truth. The fact that someone like Bethany—a cocktail waitress without any education or life—could figure it out?

Well, it pisses me off.

"We don't have to know *why* she's obsessed with you to know that she is." James settles back in his chair like he's resigned to what he's saying. "So I guess the question now is, what are you going to do about it?"

"Me? Just me?"

"We." He cocks an eyebrow at me. "But if you'd stopped blogging like I asked, then this wouldn't be a problem."

"You think I don't know that? I'm well aware of the fact that I brought this on our family." My head hurts, and I rub my temples, closing my eyes so I can try to concentrate. "You know what, let's not fight. She's crazy, James, but that doesn't mean we need to let her come between us. Help me. Please. I'm sorry about all of this, but you have to help me."

He's silent, and I keep my eyes closed, not wanting to look at his face while he thinks through what we need to do next. I have a very good feeling I know what he's thinking.

If we had just called social services when we found Knox instead of taking him, then Bethany wouldn't have any leverage over us.

If I had stopped blogging and using social media the way I have been, then I wouldn't have slipped up, and she wouldn't have found a way to hurt our family.

This is all on me, it's all my fault, but we could both go down for it. That means he's going to help me however he can. I'm sure of it.

James loves me and the kids and his job. There's no way he'll want to risk losing any of what he's worked so hard for just because Bethany is crazy and has picked me to stalk.

"Are you going to humor her for a bit? See if she gets bored? I know that doesn't sound like fun," he says, correctly interpreting the expression on my face, "but you can't just cut ties with her right now. She'd go straight to the police, and then we'd lose everything."

"I don't want to pretend to be friends with her," I say, but I know my husband is correct. As much as I'd like to cut her out of my life, call the cops and get a restraining order, and never see her again, that would be the most dangerous thing I could possibly do. It's better for me to go along with what she wants, or at least pretend that I am.

"I know you don't," he says, and there's an edge to his voice that wasn't there a moment ago. "But what choice do you really think that you have? You opened up your life to this woman, and now she found out our secret. You have to pretend to be friends with her. See if she gets bored."

"But she won't." I slap my hands down on the chair's arms, the sound loud in the room. It stings my palms, and tears burn my eyes, but the pain feels good, so I do it again. "That's the thing, James, she isn't going to stop. She has nothing in her life, and now that she thinks she has something, why would she give it up?"

"Do you know that? Did she say that?"

"No, but you didn't talk to her, James. She's pathetic. She has a crap job and no friends, and I bet she has a shitty little apartment where she lives by herself. Hell, she has no kids, no family, and she's obsessed with a mommy blogger. What the hell am I supposed to do about that?"

I don't even realize that my voice is getting louder and louder until I stop talking and hear the sound of little feet coming towards me. Turning, my mouth falls open when I see Penelope hovering in the doorway, her pajama pants twisted around her waist, her thumb automatically going up to her mouth.

Sucking her thumb is a terrible habit and one we have mostly broken her of, but she still does it when she gets really stressed out.

"Mommy?" Her voice quivers.

I throw the blanket to the side to go to her. "Hey, darling," I say, pulling her into a hug. "What are you doing awake? Couldn't sleep?"

"I heard you slamming things," she says, and I close my eyes, immediately regretting hitting the chair arms, no matter how good it felt at the time. "I thought something was wrong."

"Nothing's wrong." Turning so I can look at James, I eyeball him, trying to decide if we've talked through this enough tonight. I really just want to get to bed, and then we can see what else can be done in the morning.

He catches my eye and rises, coming over to kiss Penelope on the top of her head. "Scurry along, honey," he tells her. "Your mom and I are going to lock up down here, and then she'll come tuck you in."

Our daughter hesitates, but finally pulls away from me, hurrying out of the room and up the stairs. It's only when we hear her footsteps on the stairs that I turn to look at James.

"There has to be some other way. Can't you think of something to do other than pretending to be her friend?" It's the only thing I know to ask, even though I don't think there's an answer. At least, there might not be an answer I like.

"You need to play her game," he tells me, grabbing my arm so I can't pull away from him. "Make her think the two of you are friends, make her think everything is fine. She'll get bored."

"And if she doesn't?"

He's silent, and I close my eyes, not wanting to look at him while he thinks about what the two of us are going to do. I don't want to see the expression on his face as he tries to think it through, don't want to imagine what's going through his head.

"If she doesn't get bored and leave you alone, then the two of us will have to stop this," he finally says.

I look at him, waiting for more.

"I'm not losing my family to some cocktail waitress," he continues. "We'll do whatever it takes to stop that from happening."

23

BETHANY

I don't get to see Eliza again until Saturday morning. What I need is a new job that will allow me to have nights off so I can go over to her house when James is home, and we can all hang out, or so that Eliza and I can hit the town, and he can stay home with the kids. It's frustrating to have to work around so many people's schedules when Eliza and I are such good friends.

But it's because I care about her so much that I'm willing to do whatever I can to accommodate her when we hang out. Sure, I'd love to just move on into her house so we can be together all the time, but she's not quite ready for that yet. I planted the seed for her when I asked about a guest room in her house, but she didn't pick up on what I was asking.

That's okay. She will in time.

It's just silly to make me continue to live here in my little apartment when she and her family have that huge house with so much room in it for all of us. There's no reason for me to live away from Eliza, not when the two of us are going to start spending so much time together.

That's something I want to talk to her about today. I know

she'll be cautious at first, because she has to think about the safety of her kids, but I get it. I respect that she wants to keep Penelope and Knox safe, and so do I. That's why I didn't immediately go to the police when I found out the truth about Knox.

I could have, and that's something she needs to remember. I could ruin her and James, but that's not what I want. I just want to be her friend, just want to have a relationship with her kids, just want to be part of her perfect life. I know mine isn't anything like hers, but that doesn't mean she can't let me in and let me enjoy some of what it's like to be her.

Glancing in the mirror, I swipe a bit of lipstick on before tucking stray strands of hair behind my ears. I look... well, not great, not as put-together as Eliza does, but pretty good. This lipstick is old, but it made me so nervous stealing it that I haven't ever been back to the store to try to get another one.

But Eliza can take me shopping. She'll offer to pay for everything, and at first I'll refuse, because that's what good friends do, but when she pushes it and tells me she really wants to pay for my items, I'll let her.

It's the right thing to do. She owes me for keeping her secret a secret.

When I'm sure I look my best, I lock up my apartment, jiggling the lock out of habit to make sure it won't pop open if someone were to try it, then hurry out to my car, keeping my head down so I won't have to speak to anyone.

I can't wait to move in with Eliza.

The drive goes by quickly. In no time at all I'm standing on her front porch. After ringing the doorbell, I try the door, but I'm disappointed to find it locked. "She doesn't have to lock me out," I mutter, shifting my feet back and forth while I wait for someone to open it.

Maybe it will be Penelope. I bet she'll like the little doll I picked up for her from work. A customer's kid dropped her doll during dinner, and even though they called later and asked if anyone had seen it, I lied and said it was gone. It's cute and almost looks new, so I'm sure Penelope will be grateful.

Or it could be James. He's so handsome, and even though I wouldn't ever cheat with my friend's husband, that doesn't mean I can't enjoy how easy he is on the eyes. After we hang out a little bit more and he gets to know my personality, I want to ask him if he has any single friends he can introduce me to.

Fingers crossed it'll be a doctor.

A moment later, Eliza opens the door, barely swinging it open wide enough to squeeze through before she shuts it behind her and looks at me. "Hi, Bethany. It's good to see you."

I'm a little miffed that she didn't invite me right in to see her family, but maybe I'll get to come in later. "That's not how friends say hello," I say, grabbing her and pulling her into a hug.

She resists for a moment, but then relaxes.

I squeeze her tight before letting her go and attempting to air-kiss her cheeks. I've seen some women at the Tipsy Cat do that, and they always look incredibly fancy when they do.

Eliza's cheeks are flushed when she steps back, and she adjusts her purse before glancing down at what I have in my hand.

"What is that?" Her nose wrinkles a little.

"Oh, I brought Penelope a doll." Grinning, I hold it up for Eliza to see. "Is she right inside? I can hand it to her."

"I'll give it to her." Eliza takes the doll from me and stuffs it in her purse. I want to argue with her that Penelope needs to know it came from me, but there's a set to Eliza's jaw that I don't really like. She takes a deep breath before looking at me. "What did you want to do today?"

"Shopping." I announce the word and then loop my arm through hers. "And I thought I'd drive. It took a while, but I made sure to clean out my car before coming to get you so it would be nice and clean. Where do you want to go?"

"Um, I'm fine with whatever. Did you have anything in particular you wanted? We could just go to that one store and then be done."

I stop in my tracks and turn to look at her. "Do you not want to go shopping with me?"

Eliza's eyes open wide, and her mouth falls open. "What? No, of course I do. Why would you say that?"

"Because you suggested just going to one store and then being done." I eyeball her, trying to tell if she's being honest with me. I thought the two of us were really looking forward to this day. She told me Saturday was the best day for her to hang out this week, not only because of my work schedule, but because it meant James would be home with the kids, so we could do whatever we wanted to.

"Oh, I didn't mean it like that." She sounds nervous. "I just didn't want you to get bored, because I wasn't sure if shopping was really your thing."

"I won't get bored," I tell her, laughing. "I'll be with my best friend. What else could I possibly want?" We reach my car, and I open the door for her, which feels a little awkward, but it also seems like a great way to help her become a little more at ease. By the time we're pulling out of her driveway, I can feel that she's relaxed some.

"So are you going to blog about this?" It feels a little strange to ask Eliza that, but I want to know. I made sure to look my best when leaving the apartment, so I would fit right in when she took any pictures for her blog later.

"Blog about it?" She frowns and looks over at me. Her purse is resting on her lap, her hands on top of it. I notice how stiff her back is, how her feet are flat on the floorboard of the car. "Why would I blog about it?"

Frustration rises in me, but I tamp it down. "It's our first trip out as best friends. Why wouldn't you?"

"Because I blog about mommy things." She speaks slowly, like she's not sure if I'm going to understand what she's saying.

But I do. I hear the words, and I understand them perfectly. "You don't think that trying to make friends as a mom and then finding a new friend is worth a blog post? I know you wrote about it before, how hard it can be to find friends when you're so busy being a parent and how lonely it can be when you're doing it all by yourself. Why else do you think I'm here?"

"It's different," she begins, but then stops. "You're right. It is hard to find friends as a parent, but our friendship is so new that it would be strange to write about it, don't you think? Let's see where it goes."

"What does that mean?" I've driven quickly, and I pull smoothly into a parking space in front of the mall. "*See where it goes.* I know where I want our friendship to go, don't you?"

"Of course I do." She reaches over and lightly touches the back of my hand. I didn't realize how hard I was squeezing the steering wheel until she does. "It's just new and exciting, and sometimes it's nice to keep things like that private. You know?"

"Like Knox."

She stiffens. "Something like that. A little different."

"But not totally. It's the same, because you don't want anyone to take him away. And you don't want anyone to take away this friendship." I wag my finger between the two of us.

She nods, and I feel myself relax. "Right. You get it, Bethany. I knew you would. Now, let's go see what we can find shopping and maybe get something to eat, how does that sound?"

"Sounds good. I want to make sure we snap a cute picture for Instagram, and then I want to talk to you about your guest room. Nobody's staying there, and your place is nicer than my apartment, so I thought I could move in. What do you think? It could be like college, except I can help out by watching the kids while you work." I smile at her.

Her face grows pale, and she presses her mouth into a tight line before she gets out of the car, slamming the door and then wiping her hands on her jeans.

Eliza not answering me is not the most frustrating thing about this little interaction. What bothers me the most is that what she wants to do today does sound fun, and I want to spend the time with her. More than her avoiding answering my question about me moving in, though, she's lying to me, and I know it.

She doesn't want to keep me hidden away because she's scared someone will take me like they would take Knox. She wants to keep me hidden away because she doesn't want anyone to know we're friends.

I'm not letting her hide our friendship.

24

ELIZA

The only good thing about shopping with Bethany is that I don't have to come up with much to say, because she's been keeping up an almost constant stream of conversation without me having to say much at all. She talks about herself all the time, like she's trying to prove to me that the two of us will be friends, agrees with everything I say, and is one hundred percent obsessed with me.

I shiver as I follow her through the mall, weaving around groups of teenagers and some happy couples. My arms hurt from where her shopping bags are cutting into them, but I don't want to complain because I think we're about finished in here. Honestly, how many more stores can she stop at and expect me to be willing to foot the bill?

It happened so quickly the first time that I'm not even sure how it happened. She was checking out at a clothing store and turned to me, a grin on her face, asking if I could float her a loan. Even though I really didn't want to, I swiped my card, thinking that it would be just one purchase and then we could get out of there, and I could pretend this wasn't happening.

But then she just expected me to keep paying, and I honestly wasn't sure how to stop. That's how I've managed to ring up a couple of hundred dollars on my credit card, and none of it is for me.

I'm barely able to worry about the amount I'm ringing up on my credit card because I keep thinking about what she said about moving into my guest room.

Who the hell does she think she is? James would never agree to it, even if I wanted her to move in, which I don't.

The thought of her right down the hall from me—from the kids—scares me. She's so pushy; how in the world would I know what she would do?

We're about to reach the doors that lead out into the parking lot when I hear someone call my name. Keeping my face turned resolutely to the door, I hope they won't chase me down or call again, but a moment later I hear my name, then feel a hand on my shoulder.

I stop, not really wanting to see who chased me down in the mall, but Bethany is also turning around, a smile on her face as she prepares herself to meet my friend.

"Eliza! Look at you, shopping until you drop. I swear, it's so good to see you out and about." Nicole Harding, the wife of one of James' co-workers, hugs me, then steps back, glancing at Bethany as she pushes her way closer to the two of us to join the conversation.

In this moment, I see Bethany through Nicole's eyes, and I cringe. Her hair is mousy and limp, the lipstick color she chose much too bright for her pale complexion. She looks like she's trying too hard, and the way she positions herself next to me, moving closer than I would have liked, makes me want to scream.

"Nicole, it's so good to see you," I say, shifting the bags a little on my arms to keep them from completely cutting off circulation. "This is my friend Bethany."

"*Best* friend," Bethany corrects, grinning at Nicole, who looks surprised. "Eliza and I have had the most amazing day shopping, and now we're about to head back to her house to spend some time with the kids."

"Kids?" Nicole tilts her head as she repeats the word and looks at me.

"Kid," I correct firmly. "One kid and also James. Sometimes Bethany and I call them my *kids* as a joke. You know how husbands can be."

Nicole laughs, but her eyes flick to Bethany and then back to me like she's not entirely sure she believes the joke.

I hold my breath until Nicole laughs.

"Tell me about it! Brent can be so needy sometimes that it's like we have a third one crawling around, and nobody to help me. Anyway, tell everyone I said hello. You two have fun shopping." She glances again at Bethany, and I can practically see the questions she wants to ask written all over her face.

How did the two of you meet?

What in the world do you have in common?

Are you sure you really want to be spending time with someone who dresses like this?

"Tell Brent I said hello," I say, trying to wiggle my fingers at her before Bethany opens the door, and I follow her outside. Besides a few mall employees taking their smoke break twenty feet away, we're alone, and I turn on the woman next to me. "Why in the world would you make a slip like that?"

Bethany grins, but there's no humor behind her smile. "You did a good job covering up, Eliza. You're quick."

"Not funny. You know nobody can know about Knox." I'm keeping my voice low and calm, when really all I want to do is scream at Bethany for putting me in this position. "You did that on purpose."

Her smile fades, and I feel my stomach drop. "You can't prove that, and even if you could, what would it prove? It was a slip of the tongue, that's all."

I need to stop pushing things with her and I know it, but right now, I'm seeing red. I just went on a shopping spree for this woman, and she tried to throw me under the bus with someone I know. Dropping the bags down to the sidewalk, I rotate my wrists to get some feeling back in my arms and stare at her.

"It wasn't a slip of the tongue, Bethany. Why did you do it?"

There's a little voice in the back of my head screaming at me that I'm being stupid and that I need to just drop this and let it go, but I can't. Everything I've ever done since bringing Knox home has been to keep him safe. I'm not about to let it all fall apart because of this woman.

"Fine." Her voice cuts. "You want to know why I did it? To remind you that we're friends, Eliza, and that we're going to stay friends. I know you didn't want to come shopping with me all day long, but you did it anyway. Why is that?"

I know the answer she wants, but I honestly don't want to give it to her. Swallowing hard, I force myself to look her in the eyes. "Because we're friends."

"That's right." She smiles. "We're friends. And we're going to stay friends. You needed one, and I wanted one. Do you understand?"

I think I do. I think I understand that Bethany has lost the plot, and I'm honestly a little worried about what she might do if I try to turn her down or tell her I don't want to be her friend. I didn't want to be her friend from the moment I met her, but she's made it very clear to me that I don't have much of a choice.

"I understand," I force myself to say.

"Good." She gives a little squeal like she's a lot younger

than she really is, but then looks serious again. "I think you have a lovely family, Eliza, and I want to respect that. But I need you to understand that it can all be taken away. All of it. I know your secret about Knox, and I don't think you want anyone finding out the truth, do you?"

I shake my head. My entire body feels cold, and I know the chills are just because I know she's right. As much as I hate to admit it, or even consider the possibility, Bethany has information that could destroy my entire family if she were to decide to share it with anyone. All I can do is hope that she doesn't.

Which means I need to keep her happy.

"I'm just so glad we're friends," I say, but my mouth feels stiff, and I have to force myself to smile at her. If Bethany notices that I seem a little off, she doesn't remark on it, just grins at me, and helps me pick up the bags I put on the ground.

"Me too, Eliza. Friendship like this doesn't come around very often, but you can bet that when it does, it's worth the fight to keep it." Her voice is light and happy, but each of her words settles heavily in my stomach.

I'm silent on the way home, but I don't think Bethany notices. She's too busy chatting about all the new clothes I bought her, and what she wants to do this week. I know I should respond, or at least acknowledge that she's speaking, but all I can do is stare out the windshield.

I might look quiet, but inside, my mind is working a mile a minute.

I have to get rid of my new friend.

25

BETHANY

After dropping Eliza back off at her house, I head home, taking my time on the curvy roads and stopping for longer than necessary at the stop signs. It feels really good to move slower, to feel like I have things under control.

And it's all because Eliza has a secret that she wants to keep anyone from ever finding out.

"This is great!" I can't help the words that spill from my lips as I pull into the parking lot in front of my apartment building. Who cares that the place looks like something from the set of a horror movie or that my neighbors give me the creeps? There's an expiration date on me having to live here, and I feel like it's coming up faster than I realized.

Eliza bought me so many things, all without complaining, that it takes me three trips to get everything hauled upstairs. Once I have my door locked and I drink a glass of water, I dump everything on my bed and step back to eyeball it.

New jeans. A few dresses. Plenty of tank tops and shirts. Three skirts and two pairs of sneakers. High heels and chunky platforms, which I've never bought before, because I didn't think I had a place to wear them. Even some bras and new underwear, all of it silky and soft with cute little details like bows that will make me feel fancy while I'm wearing them.

I want to try on some of my new clothes, but before I do that, I sit on the bed and grab my phone, navigating to Instagram so I can check on what Eliza posted. She made a big stink about not posting on her mommy blog about the two of us becoming friends, which I don't love, but she did tell me she'd post on Instagram.

I hope it's one of the selfies the two of us took in fitting rooms. She kept telling me she was happy to wait outside the room for me, but I wanted her in there with me like a real friend, so I told her I wanted her to help me if I got stuck with a zipper.

"She posted," I say, tapping on the first square on her page. Excitement rushes through me when I think about making it onto her Instagram twice in a week, but it quickly fades when the little square grows to take up the entire screen.

She posted, but she didn't post with me in it. I feel anger, hot and fast, rush through me when I realize I'm not staring at a selfie of the two of us, our faces pressed together, matching grins on display for the camera, but one of her and Penelope.

Eliza's crouching behind Penelope, her arms around the little girl, their faces next to each other as they both grin at the camera. It's the first time all day I've seen Eliza look this happy, and the fact that I wasn't the one who was able to make her smile like that really burns.

Then my eyes flick down to the caption.

The happiest moment of any day is getting to come home to this sweet girl. #momlife #mommyblogger #bestfriends

"Best. Friends." I exhale, the sound explosive, then immediately exit Instagram and dial Eliza. She'd better pick up. She has a lot of explaining to do, and I can't wait to hear how she tries to weasel her way out of this one.

"Hi, Bethany," Eliza says.

I force myself to take a deep breath so I can answer her. "Where's our post on your Instagram?"

"What?" She sounds confused, but I'm not going to be deterred. I know what I saw on her page, and she has to know that posting that picture with Penelope instead of with me was going to upset me. "What are you talking about?"

"I wanted you to post about our fun day, Eliza. I wanted everyone to see that we were good friends, but you posted with Penelope."

"Well, yeah, it was a really cute picture, and the two of us have a lot of fun together. What in the world are you so upset about, Bethany? We had a good day together, right? You got everything you wanted, I bought you whatever you looked twice at, so I don't know what you're complaining about." There's an edge to her voice I don't like.

"You're my best friend," I say, and even though I know I'd laugh at someone else getting this worked up over a mother's relationship with her daughter, I can't help it. "I want to be in your posts. Remember that I know your secret."

"Jesus, fine. I'll make another one. You don't have to threaten something like that." Her voice drops, and I imagine her covering the phone and turning away from Penelope to keep her daughter from hearing what's being said. "I did what you wanted today. You can't keep making threats like that, Bethany. This has to end eventually."

"It doesn't." I feel brave saying those words to her. "It doesn't, Eliza, and you know it. I'm in control. Now, post the picture, make it look like we had a great time, and I want to come for dinner tomorrow night. With the kids. Both of them."

Now's the time to remind Eliza that I'm the one who holds all the power here. She might have fans and readers who cling on her every word, but she's my friend.

She hesitates, and while I'm sure she's just thinking through her options and deciding what she's going to say to me, I don't like that she thinks she can pause for that long without agreeing to what I just told her I want her to do.

"Eliza, remember what I could do to you. To James. Who do you think would get custody of Penelope? Do you think she'd end up in foster care like you did when you were younger? Can you imagine? Would she be able to survive it?"

Eliza lets out a hiss, and I smile.

Got her.

"You wouldn't really do anything to my family, would you?" There's doubt in her voice. I hear it, and I love it. I want her to be afraid of me, to know that I will do anything I have to in order to get the life I want. It's not fair that someone like Eliza can have the perfect life just because of how she looks or who her husband is.

Why shouldn't I have the same chance at a perfect life?

"I'll do whatever it takes to get what I want, Eliza. I want to be your friend. It's not that hard." Without giving her a chance to respond, I hang up the phone.

I'm honestly not interested in hearing any excuses she might try to come up with. Eliza and I are meant to be friends, no matter what she might think, and the sooner she understands that and makes the effort to meet me halfway in our friendship, the sooner she and I can have more fun.

Flopping down on my bed, I lean back among my bags of clothes she bought for me. It was really nice having her all to myself today and knowing that anything I wanted her to buy, she would. I liked that.

But it's still not enough. Today was a test, just something to make sure Eliza wasn't going to try to back out of what I wanted her to do. I had to make sure she would be willing to go as far as I needed her to. Tomorrow will be nice, having dinner with her family, and that will be a good time for me to bring up what I really want from her.

Eliza's going to completely change my life.

Whether she wants to or not.

26

ELIZA

I'm so mad I can't speak.

James stares at me from across the kitchen, where he's busy putting together a snack for Penelope and Knox, and even though part of me feels like I should help him to make sure the kids each get their favorite things on the plate he's putting together, I can't move from where I'm standing.

As soon as Bethany hung up on me, I dropped my phone to the counter, planted my hands on either side of it, and forced myself to take deep breaths as I tried to calm down.

It didn't work.

"Eliza? Darling? Are you okay?" Leaving the apple he was slicing up on the cutting board, James hurries to my side, then bands his arm around my waist to support me. "What's happening?"

"It's *her*." Right now, I don't even want to say her name.

"Bethany?"

I nod. "She wants to come over for dinner tomorrow. In fact, she *invited* herself. Said that we had to have her over, or she would tell about Knox."

James pulls away from me, his gaze serious. "What?"

"She wouldn't," I say, but even as the words leave my lips, I'm not sure if I'm right or not. Didn't she just freak out over me posting a picture on Instagram of me with my daughter instead of with her? Who knows how crazy the woman is and what she's willing to do. I have no idea how far she's willing to take this.

"Can you guarantee that? Can you guarantee he'll be safe —that *we'll* be safe? Eliza, this is exactly what I knew would happen." He slaps his hands down on his thighs and sighs, bending over and sucking in air.

"This is what you knew would happen?" Even though I know getting angry at my husband isn't going to solve anything, I don't want him to be able to make this all about him. "When we saved Knox from that hellhole, you thought for sure some psycho stalker would blackmail us? Please, James."

"This wouldn't have happened if you hadn't been so damn hardheaded about it all." James turns to me, and for the first time, I notice the paring knife still in his hand.

"About what? Taking Knox? *Saving* Knox?"

"And your blog." James shakes his head, then looks down at his hand like he's surprised he's still holding the knife. Carefully, like he thinks it might bite him, he puts it on the counter. "She found you through your blog, and if you had just stopped writing it, stopped with the social media when I asked you to, we wouldn't be going through this right now."

We've had this conversation before, and I don't know how to get him to see that I'm not the issue here. I hate the idea of him turning on me and believing that I'm the problem, even though I feel incredibly guilty about the entire thing. I know this is my fault, but to hear my husband say it almost brings me to my knees.

"Bethany is the problem, not me. She's insane, James. We

were happy; we were fine. I slipped up about Knox, but she's the one threatening us."

"You can say that, but you need to fix this, Eliza. What are you going to do? Just let her make you do whatever she wants?"

I'm not sure. I can't take my eyes away from the knife. It's right by my phone, and what I really want to do right now is stab it into my phone, through the case, and destroy it.

But if I did that, I'd lose everything. My fans, my readers, all the people I've tried so hard to make a connection with. James may not like the fact that I have so many readers who love me, but I do, and I'm not about to throw them all away over someone like Bethany. She can't take what I've worked so hard to build.

"I don't know what to do," I admit, forcing myself to look James in the eyes. What I see there terrifies me.

I hoped I would see compassion. I really hoped I would look at my husband, at the man I promised to love for the rest of my life, and I would see him caring for me, hoping that things were going to work out, willing to do whatever it took to protect our family.

But that's not what I see.

For the first time since I met James, I see anger in his eyes as he looks at me.

"She's going to hurt our family."

"I'm sorry," I say, but he shakes his head.

"Sorry's not going to cut it, Eliza. We need to stop her. *You* need to stop her."

I freeze in place. As much as I'd love to argue with him, I know he's right. I want to rail against him, to tell him he doesn't understand—but I have to fix this. None of this would have happened if I hadn't pushed him to take Knox and bring him home.

Scratch that.

None of this would have happened if Camilla hadn't been such a horrible person. James is upset with me, and I understand that he's looking for someplace to put the blame of what's going on, but he's placing it on me, and I'm not the person he should be angry at.

He should be mad at Camilla. The problem with that is, she's not here in front of him, and I am, and so of course he's going to take his anger out on me. I don't have to like it for it to make sense. I just have to figure out how I'm going to get him to calm down, what I need to say to make him stop looking at me like he is right now.

"We can fix this," I tell him, reaching out and lightly touching his arm. I love my husband, and even though I'm frustrated that he's angry with me and not with my sister, I'm not going to hold that against him. He's panicked right now, and I understand that. "*I* can fix this, James, okay? You have to trust me. Don't let Bethany turn us against each other. I don't want to fight with you about this. I don't want her to come between us. You and I can face anything together, James. We just have to be on the same page."

He exhales hard, and I feel myself relax a little bit. I was worried there for a minute that he was going to turn on me, but we're a team.

We just have to stay that way.

James stares at me and then gives his head a tired little shake, like he's just as tired of this conversation as I am. "How are you going to fix this? She knows about Knox. She's willing to hold that over your head to get whatever she wants. Tell me, Eliza, what in the world do you think you could do to this woman that would make her back off?"

I think about all the money I spent on her at the mall today. I think about how eager she was for me to pull out my credit card and swipe it at every store. She didn't ask questions like she really wanted to get to know me. It was more like she was picking me apart, to find something she could use against me.

The thought of what I might need to do to protect my family terrifies me, and I don't want to let myself entertain it, but it's there, snaking through my brain, a quiet voice whispering.

I don't know if I can ignore it.

There's something evil in Bethany, and I know what you have to do to get rid of evil things.

You have to kill them.

27

BETHANY

I'm surprisingly calm as I stand on Eliza's front porch and wait for her to open the door. After ringing the doorbell, I thought about just opening the door and letting myself in, but I have a very good feeling she and James wouldn't appreciate that.

We're good friends, but we're not that close yet. Soon, though, I have a feeling she's going to offer me a key to her house. I'll be able to just pop by whenever I want to see her or the kids, and it'll be great. Not only will I be able to come by when I want to, but if she needs anything, she can call, and I can swing it over without her having to come to the door.

It's going to be great.

And then I'm going to move in.

I'm not sure when it's going to happen, only that I'm convinced it will.

After another moment, during which I smooth down the front of the new shirt Eliza bought me and clear my throat to try to get rid of any remaining nervousness, the door swings open.

It's James.

"James," I cry, holding my arms out for a hug. "Thank you so much for having me over for dinner!"

He doesn't move to hug me, but that's fine. I step in through the open door and wrap my arms around him, pulling him to me, even though he doesn't reciprocate. Sure, it's rude that he won't hug me back, but maybe he's just worried Eliza would see and get jealous.

I'll have to make it clear to them that I don't want her husband. James is nice, but I'm not interested in him.

I just want to be friends with his wife.

After hugging him for a moment and breathing in the smell of his expensive cologne, I finally let him go and step back. "I'm really excited to be here. It was so kind of Eliza to invite me."

This makes him blink, like he wasn't expecting me to say that. "I thought you invited yourself."

I laugh, then slap him on the arm like I haven't heard anything that funny in a long time. "James, you crack me up. Eliza and I are just so close, you know? Who really knows who invited who? Now, where are the kids? I can't wait to say hello to them."

James is silent as he closes and locks the front door. I ignore how rude he's being as I walk down the hall to the kitchen. Whatever Eliza is cooking for dinner smells amazing, and I pause in the doorway to watch as she stirs something at the stove, then bends down to open the oven and glance inside.

"Smells delicious," I say, coming up behind her.

Eliza whips around, a smile on her face.

Good. I'm glad to see her looking happy about me being here. I know she wasn't thrilled yesterday when I told her I wanted her to make an Instagram post of the two of us hanging out shopping, but she did what I asked.

I knew she'd come around.

"Thanks." She brushes her bangs out of her eyes with the back of her hand. "It's nothing too crazy, just a roast chicken with veggies, gravy and some bread. Oh, and I made brownies for dessert. Penelope helped."

"Knox didn't want to?" I smile at Eliza, enjoying how it feels to make her remember that I know about her second child, the son she's not supposed to have. I fully intend on seeing him at some point tonight.

Maybe I'll get a selfie with him on my phone just for insurance.

Just so I can prove he exists.

"He's not huge on cooking," Eliza says over her shoulder as she gets plates down from a cupboard. "Here, will you please put these on the table?"

I take the plates from her, square white ones that look incredibly modern, then frown when I count how many there are. "Only three? Do the kids have their own plates? Plastic ones, maybe?" I know Eliza hates using plastic in the house with her family, but I also know that sometimes kids can be really picky about things.

"Oh, Penelope and Knox aren't eating with us." Eliza still has her back to me. She's now digging napkins out of a drawer. I watch as she tosses them on the counter, pulls out three sets of silverware, then picks it all up and turns to look at me. "Is there are problem with the plates?"

This isn't how it was supposed to go.

"I wanted Knox and Penelope to join us," I say, still holding the plates tight so I don't drop them. "I wanted this to be a family dinner."

Eliza stares at me like she can't believe what I'm saying, then gives her head a little shake. "They're upstairs watching a movie and eating pizza. I offered them the chance to sit with us, but they don't want to."

"I want them to." How hard is this for Eliza to understand? I wanted the kids to join us so the five of us could all eat together. How in the world am I supposed to be Eliza's best friend if her kids won't even sit and eat with me?

This isn't how *any* of this was supposed to go. Eliza hasn't made an effort to become my friend. I honestly feel like I'm the one taking all the steps towards her, doing what I can to reach out to her. I don't know why she won't meet me halfway.

"Bethany, sorry, but they didn't want to join us."

Should I continue to push this? I can hear my heartbeat; I'm so stressed out just watching Eliza stare at me. It's wrong that she could ruin my night like this by changing things without permission, but I'm not sure how hard to push back on her.

Sure, I could get her to get the kids down here, but what if they threw a fit? I want them to like me, not hate me for making their mealtime stressful.

"Fine," I say, gritting my teeth into a smile and forcing my legs to carry me across the room to the table. "I'm sure I'll get to see them before I leave, don't you think?"

She exhales hard and joins me at the table, tucking the napkins under the edge of the plates, then arranging the silverware so it's perfect.

"I'm sure they'll say goodnight," she finally says, then walks back to the stove.

I eyeball the table. It's rectangular, and we set two plates on one side across from a single one on the other. That was my doing, because I want to sit right by Eliza. James can join us, of course. I don't have a problem with him being around, and I'm sure he's a nice enough guy.

Eliza moves quickly, getting everything out of the oven and in serving dishes, then puts it all on the table, pointing behind her at the sink. "Go wash up, and I'll get James."

I let the water run hot before putting my hands under it,

then enjoy her lemon foaming soap as I suds up. I know I'm taking longer than necessary to wash my hands, but it feels really good to use such nice soap. The fluffy towel next to the sink doesn't hurt, either.

But then I walk back into the dining room and see James and Eliza sitting at the table together, and my heart sinks.

He's in my spot, right next to her. Do I say something? Do I ask him to move?

She's looking at me with a triumphant expression, and I slip into the seat across from them, suddenly feeling like I'm at an interview and I don't know any of the questions they're going to ask.

"Thank you for joining us tonight, Bethany," James says, reaching out to take my plate to serve me my meal. "It's always nice to meet my wife's friends."

His words make me glow. Even though, just a moment ago, I was a little angry at him for sitting in my seat, the fact that he recognizes that Eliza and I are friends makes me relax some. I take my plate back, put some bread on it by the chicken, then pass the basket across the table.

"I'm so excited to have found someone I love spending so much time with," I tell him. I have no idea if Eliza's told him the truth—that I know about Knox and what they did. It's difficult for me to read James, but the smile he gives me makes me feel more confident that he must not know anything.

"Well, you certainly do want to spend a lot of time together," Eliza says, and I shoot her a look. "I don't mind it, but I think we need to come up with a better balance of how often to see each other. I just don't want to be away from my kids too much."

"That's why I wanted to have dinner here tonight," I explain. "I thought we could hang out and see the kids."

She nods and takes a bite of chicken, but doesn't answer.

I need her to see that I'm doing this for her. "I know you said the kids had their own dinner, but if they joined us, then we could hang out, and you could still be spending time with them as their mom."

"Really? I could still be a mom?" Eliza puts her fork down and stares at me. "Why in the world do you think I want to be friends with you, Bethany? We're nothing alike. Why me? Why would you choose me, out of everyone in the world you could be friends with? What is it about me?"

I haven't even had a bite of dinner, and even though it smells so good my mouth is watering, I can't take my eyes off the woman across from me. She looks livid. Her chest rises and falls, and James reaches over, lightly rubbing her back, helping her calm down.

Why is he comforting *her*? I'm the one who isn't wanted here.

"We're friends," I say slowly, wanting to make sure I get through to her, "because we're so much alike."

"We're not, though. I'm a stay-at-home mom and successful blogger, and you work in a bar. How are we alike?"

"It's not about what we do, Eliza. It's about who we are."

She gasps, but doesn't respond.

Encouraged, I continue, "We're both survivors. We both know how to get what we want, and we both want more than what we had. Neither one of us is afraid to reach out and take something if we think it will help us reach our goals later in life. That's how we're the same—not because of what we do, but because of who we are on the inside."

"Eliza isn't like that," James says, finally coming to his wife's aid. I slowly turn to look at him.

"No?" When he shakes his head, I grin, then continue, "Because what would you call it when she was willing to take Knox even though it wasn't legal? What about running the blog and spending all her time working on that? You can't tell me you didn't once wish that she was available more often, can you?"

He stares at me.

Eliza lets out a soft hiss from between her clenched teeth. "Why are you doing this?"

"I want what you have. I want to be your friend." Grabbing my fork for the first time since we sat down, I stab it through the air at her to get my point across. "All I've wanted from the beginning was for you to be my friend, for you to let me into your perfect life."

"And if I don't?"

She's braver than I thought; I'll give her that.

Or dumber.

"If you don't, then you'll say goodbye to Knox. To Penelope. To James. Someone else would raise them, would kiss their booboos, would come running when they have nightmares. I'll make sure of it."

28

ELIZA

"She's insane," I tell James, pulling back the covers and slipping into bed next to him. We both showered after dinner, him first and then me. I stood under the spray until the hot water ran out, and it felt like it was sleeting on my bare skin. "What the hell are we going to do?"

He's silent, and I think for a moment that there's no way he fell asleep this fast. Still... Reaching over, I touch his shoulder, and he flops onto his back, his eyes locked on mine.

"You brought her into our house," he tells me, and the dull sound of his voice makes me shiver. "You tell me, Eliza, what the hell do you think we should do about her?"

I don't know. That's the problem.

Bethany terrifies me. The way she acts like the two of us are close friends and how she wants to be around my children scares me to no end. I can't handle the thought of her near my babies, but that's what she wants.

And even worse, she thinks we're the same.

"Please, James," I say, cupping his cheek. "I don't know what to do."

"She's not going to stop, is she?" His voice is tight. "Not until she's a part of our lives, not until she has everything she wants."

"I think she just wants to be my friend. She said she just wants to be my friend." My mind races as I think about what else she might want from me, and I take a deep breath. "But we have to come up with a way to make her stop. I'm sure we can, James. The two of us together, we can come up with something. There has to be something we can say to her to make her back off. I just don't know yet what it is."

"And if you can't figure out what to say?" Shifting position, James sits up, then props his pillow behind his back so he can settle into it. He stares at me, and I let my hand fall from his face. "You think you can come up with something that will make her stop, but what if you're wrong?"

"I don't know." My mouth feels dry when I think about what she might do to my family if she doesn't get what she wants. Seeing her earlier tonight with Knox, seeing her hold his shoulder so she could pull him closer to him... it almost made me lose my mind.

"You need to have an idea. You're the one who got us into this, Eliza. What are you willing to do to get us out?"

I don't know what to say to him. I had a few thoughts run through my head during dinner, things that are too terrible to name out loud, but might be our only option.

My only option.

"We broke the law taking Knox," I say. Even admitting that about my son makes my stomach twist. "We did, and you told me we shouldn't do it, but we did it anyway to save him, because he's family. I'll do whatever it takes to save him again and to save Penelope."

I don't want to say it, but my husband does.

"You'd kill her?"

My lips clamp tight. It's the one thing I was thinking during dinner. I imagined leaping across the table at Bethany, wrapping my hands around her throat, squeezing tight as she gasped and clawed at me to stop hurting her.

I thought about it. I imagined it. I smiled thinking about saving my family in that way.

But imagining it is one thing; hearing James suggest it is another one entirely.

"Do you think we need to?" My voice is low even though the kids are both asleep and nobody is around to hear us. Bethany left a few hours ago, all smiles with her Tupperware full of leftovers. There's nobody around to hear me discuss murdering Bethany, but it still feels wrong to talk about it.

"If you can't get her to back off, then what else do you suggest? I'm not losing everything because you convinced me to kidnap our nephew and some psycho found out. You have to stop her, Eliza."

My lips are dry, and licking them doesn't help.

"You have to end this, Eliza."

I nod even though I don't want to. I feel like I'm outside my body watching this conversation. I see the intense expression on James' face, how he won't look away from me, how there's a few feet of space between us like there's an invisible force pushing us apart.

"You want me to kill her?" It's insane. *This is insane.*

There's no way my husband is asking me to do this.

No, Bethany is not my friend, but that doesn't mean I want to kill her. It doesn't mean, even though I was daydreaming about it during dinner, that I could actually go through with it.

He doesn't respond.

"I can't kill her."

"You have to stop her. You're the reason this has gone this

far, Eliza. You're the reason this woman is so obsessed with us and wants to hurt our family. You wanted Knox badly enough to kidnap him, but what are you willing to do to keep him?"

"We're in this together, you know. It's not just about what I'm willing to do to keep Knox. You have to be willing to do it, too."

"I am."

His answer is so fast, so confident, that it surprises me. I stare at him, trying to read my husband's face, but for the first time since I met him and fell in love with him, I feel like I'm looking at a stranger. I can't tell what he's thinking.

"Where do you draw the line?"

James sighs heavily and shifts the covers over him. He's going to roll over and cut the conversation off, I know it. As soon as he rolls away from me, this conversation is going to be over. If I want answers from my husband, I need to get them now.

"James. The line." I put my hand on his shoulder to stop him from moving away from me. "Where do you draw it? There has to be a line somewhere."

For a moment, I don't think he's going to answer. "There is no line, Eliza, not for our family. You did this, and you need to fix it, but I will if you're not strong enough."

Not strong enough. To what? Stop Bethany? Kill Bethany? A shiver tears through me as James closes his eyes, shutting me out. I want to grab him by the shoulders and scream into his face until he looks at me and we can discuss what this really means for us, for our family, for our kids, but I can't move.

There is no line.

There wasn't a line when we took Knox to save him, so why should there be one now? Still, the thought of killing Bethany to stop her from telling our secret makes me feel ill. I don't want to think about it, don't want it to be a possibility.

But his words hang in the air between us.
There is no line.

29

BETHANY

For the first time in a long time I'm feeling really good. My job still sucks, and I'd love to walk out of there without worrying about how I was going to pay rent after quitting, but I can't quite do that yet. Eliza hasn't offered to open up her house to me, to let me move into her guest bedroom yet.

But she will. I know she will, because I know her secret. It's amazing how just a bit of information about who a person really is, about what they do when they think nobody is looking, can suddenly be enough to make them agree to whatever you want.

So far, Eliza and I have gone shopping. I've ended up on her Instagram feed and had dinner with her and James. Now I want to take our friendship to the next level. It's crazy to think that we only met such a short while ago, but there's no reason to think our friendship will slow down anytime soon.

Not if I have anything to say about it.

James should be at work by now, so I grab my phone to fire off a quick text to Eliza, to see what she and the kids are up to this morning.

Hey, good morning! Do you and the kids want to get together and have a tea party?

I'm sure Penelope would love something like that, so it could kill two birds with one stone by letting Eliza get some shots for social media. I'll be in them, of course, so I need to make sure to wear something cute that will help me really stand out. Thanks to my shopping spree, I have more than enough options, and I leave my phone on my bed while I get up and start looking through my closet.

After deciding on a cute dress with dangly earrings and chunky platforms, I sit back down and pick up my phone. Still no message from Eliza.

She knows that I want her to text me back right away when I reach out to her, so the only thing that really makes sense is if something's wrong at the house. Maybe Knox or Penelope doesn't feel great, and she's dealing with that. Maybe she overslept after James left.

Turning my phone over and over in my hands, I think about what to do, then decide that my only option is to reach out with a call. That's what a good friend would do. I need to make sure she's okay.

Her phone rings three times before I hear a little voice answer. "Hey, Penelope, it's Bethany. I wanted to talk to your mom. Is she around? Is she okay?"

"She's here," Penelope says, her voice so sweet and innocent that I can't help but grin. It's not fair of Eliza to keep these two precious kids locked away from me. They need me in their lives, and I want to be there for them. "She's in the kitchen."

"Great, will you please give her the phone?"

"Uh-huh." There's the sound of the phone being handed off, and I hear her speak again, this time sounding like she's far away: *"Momma, it's Bethany, and she wants to talk to you."*

"What did I tell you about picking up the phone? Especially if she calls." Eliza's voice is harsh and takes me by surprise. Even though the words are muffled, I can still make out what she's saying, and I stiffen.

Why wouldn't she want Penelope to pick up the phone when I called? All I wanted to do was make sure she was okay and check in on her and the kids. It doesn't make any sense, but I'm going to get to the bottom of it.

"Bethany? What do you want?" Eliza's voice is hard, with an edge to it that I don't like. "Is something wrong?"

"No, nothing's wrong. I was calling you to find out the same. You didn't answer my text." While I speak, I finger the hem of my dress and squeeze the phone tight, waiting for her response.

Did I do the wrong thing? I've never had a close friend like this before. I don't want to have messed up by reaching out and calling her.

I shake my head. No, this is what friends do. If they're worried about something, they call. If they need to check in with the other person, they don't hesitate to do that. It's not my fault Eliza's voice is tight.

I just don't like what I heard her say to Penelope.

"I'm fine," she finally says slowly. "I just don't usually check my phone in the morning. That's all. We've been having a quiet morning here, the three of us."

"I bet you would have checked it if it had been a fan on Instagram." The words leave my lips before I can stop them, but I don't regret saying what I did. I want her to know that I'm hurt, that it bothers me she didn't immediately text me back.

Now I feel foolish sitting in my dress on the edge of my bed. I feel like an idiot for thinking she would want to get together with me this morning on such short notice. I want her to want to spend time with me because she likes me, not just because she's nervous about what I might do with the information I have about Knox.

"Listen, Bethany, I had a nice time at dinner last night, but I like spending my mornings with my kids. I didn't even notice my phone going off."

It's a lie. I know it's a lie. Not only that, but I heard her warn Penelope away from answering my calls. I want to call her out on that, to make her apologize for saying such a terrible thing to Penelope, but that's something I need to do in person.

"Do you want to get together this morning or not?" I ask the question, already sure I know the answer.

Eliza sighs. "We just have so much to do this morning. I'm in the middle of laundry, and I have a blog post to write. I just don't think it's a good idea."

"Let me come help out with the kids. If you have so much work to do, then you probably won't be able to keep an eye on them, and I'm a better option than the TV. Listen, I'm already dressed, don't say no. I'll be there in half an hour, and you can have all morning to yourself, to work without distractions. Then we can make lunch and have a picnic in the backyard."

I'm on my feet now, walking to the bathroom to brush my teeth and swipe on some mascara. Eliza doesn't answer. I grab my toothbrush, banging it against the edge of the sink as I wait for her response.

"Eliza, if we're going to be friends, then you have to make an effort. I work tonight, so this is the best time for me to hang out today."

"Fine." She sounds resigned, but I ignore it.

"Great. I'll see you soon. Can't wait!" Hanging up before she can respond, I put my phone by the sink and then stare at myself in the mirror. I look tired, but that's only because my job is so stressful and has me on my feet for so many hours.

But maybe by the time my shift would have started tonight, I'll have quit.

Maybe I can convince Eliza to hire me on to be a nanny for the kids. I can live in their house with them, watch the kids, help when she needs pictures taken for her blog.

It's what a real friend would do, and that's what I am.

A real friend.

The best one Eliza is ever going to have.

30

ELIZA

I don't want Bethany in my house, and I certainly don't want her to be spending alone time with my children, but I really need to get my blog post written and up, and there's no way I can balance it all.

That's what I tell myself, although I know the real reason I'm agreeing to this is because she could destroy everything. She could ruin my family with one simple phone call, and I'm still not convinced she won't.

James would be pissed if he knew that she was going to be in our house this morning. I know what he wants me to do, and he made it clear last night that there's really only one option that he sees. There's only one outcome.

We have to get rid of Bethany.

Either I convince her to leave us alone, or he's going to get involved. I can't imagine actually killing someone, but what other option do I really have?

She has all the power in this relationship, and that simply isn't going to continue to work for me. I need to find some power over her, something I can hold over her head, something that will allow me to live my life without looking over my shoulder for her.

But what?

I've tried to find her online, but beside the Instagram profile she's used to comment on my posts, it's like she doesn't exist. I'm so used to sharing details of my life online that it's strange to me for someone not to have information readily available.

She's a ghost, and it's impossible to find grounds for blackmail on a ghost.

Penelope walks into the kitchen, Knox trailing behind her. I'm at the table nursing a cup of coffee and debating letting James know what's going on this morning, but I really don't see how that could end up in any way other than him getting angry at me.

No, this is something I have to handle on my own. I don't like keeping secrets from James, but do I really have a choice?

Not that I can see.

"Hey, guys," I say, grabbing each of my kids and pulling them to me so I can hug them. "I have a lot of work to do this morning, so I have a surprise for you! Bethany is coming over to hang out while I work on my blog post. Won't that be fun?"

Knox doesn't answer. He's not talkative on a good day, and he's been foul since he got up this morning. When I was getting frustrated at him for his attitude, I had to remind myself that everyone, adults and kids alike, can have bad days.

"But we want to hang out with you." Penelope sticks her lower lip out and pulls away from me so she can pout. "We don't want to hang out with Bethany."

"I know, but she really wants to see you guys. I have a feeling she'd love to see your new puzzle we picked up at the store. What do you think? Or maybe you three could have an animal tea party."

That's the last thing Knox will want to do, and he sticks his tongue out a little, immediately pulling it back into his mouth when I glance over at him.

"I just want you two to be nice," I say, putting a smile on my face. "Bethany is my friend, and you need to be nice to her."

"I don't want her here." Penelope is picking up on her brother's bad attitude. "I want to spend time with you, not with her."

This is getting frustrating. If it weren't for the fact that my blog post is sponsored and I promised the company I would have it written and posted today, I might push it until later, but I have to write it. I have to take some pictures, and I have to get it up by this afternoon.

And I have to figure out how I'm going to get rid of Bethany.

"I know, darling, and you're going to have me all to yourselves this afternoon, okay? Bethany won't stay all day, and when my blog post is written and online, then you'll have all of my attention."

Both of my kids are silent, and I say a word of thanks that I got them to listen. Just as I'm about to tell them how much I appreciate them doing this, the doorbell rings.

Penelope spins away from me in a whirl of tulle. "I've got it!"

Her little temper tantrum was short-lived, and even though I want to call to her to let me get the door, I instead scoop Knox up so he can't follow her. Just because Bethany knows about him doesn't mean I want everyone in the neighborhood to find out the truth. It's bad enough having one person in my life who can hold things over my head like this.

"Hi, Penelope!" Bethany's voice carries through the foyer, and I peek around the door, making sure she's alone. "I'm so glad I get to come hang out with you and play today! Are you ready for some fun?"

"Yes!" Penelope squeals.

Traitor.

At the sound of his sister's voice, Knox squirms in my arms, so I let him go, watching as he hurries through the foyer to join Penelope. I follow, still unsure of what I'm doing, but knowing full well that I don't have much of a choice.

Scratch that. I don't have a choice. At all.

Not if I want to keep Knox.

"Bethany, hi," I say, taking the door and closing it quickly so nobody will be able to see inside. "Thanks for coming over this morning to hang out with the kids. It will be nice to get some things done this morning."

"Not a problem. You know all you have to do is ask." She smiles at me, and even though I'm sure anyone looking at her would think she was just being friendly, I swear I feel a shiver run up my spine. There's something dark in this woman. Any person who would threaten a mother and her children... she's evil.

"I appreciate it." Turning from her, I rest my hands on Penelope's and Knox's heads. "Why don't you two run on upstairs to your playroom, and Bethany will be right there. I'll write up my blog as quickly as possible, so we can all spend some time together before Bethany has to go."

The kids do what I ask, leaving me alone with the woman who knows the one thing that could ruin my family. I stare at her, willing myself to stay calm.

"If you hurt them," I hear myself saying, "I will hurt you. You do understand that, right?"

The smile Bethany wore when talking to my kids fades. "Do you really think you're in a position to threaten me, Eliza? And is that something friends would do?"

"We're not friends." I'm squeezing my hands into tight

fists, my nails almost cutting into my palms. The pain feels good. Grounding.

"We are, though." Bethany sounds wounded, and for just a moment, I think her tone is fake, but then I see the real hurt in her eyes.

This woman thinks we're really friends.

"Friends don't threaten each other," I tell her. We're just a few inches apart, and I keep my voice low so it won't carry up the stairs. "Friends don't threaten to ruin the other person's life."

Her nostrils flare. "How else was I supposed to get you to notice me, Eliza? Your life is so perfect, so wonderful, and you weren't ever going to look twice at me, but I knew we could be friends. Remember what I said. We're the same. And the next time you think about telling Penelope not to pick up the phone when I call, don't. We're friends, Eliza. Act like it."

With that, she turns away from me and hurries up the stairs after my kids. I should stop her. It's insane of me to let her go be anywhere near my children, but right now, I don't feel like I have a choice.

She has me over a barrel.

She wants this relationship with me, with my kids. She's inserted herself into my life, and I don't see a way I'm going to be able to get her to leave me alone.

It's terrifying.

I look up at the ceiling, a chill running through me.

I just allowed this woman upstairs to spend time with my kids.

What the hell was I thinking?

31

BETHANY

It's my first time upstairs at Eliza's house, but I know exactly where to go thanks to the sound of the kids playing floating down the hall as soon as I reach the top of the stairs.

For a moment, I pause, looking at all of the family pictures on the walls. At first glance, this is the perfect American family. They're all smiling, all of them happy to be together. All they're missing is a dog, a big dumb animal to fill in the gaps in these pictures.

Or me.

Stopping in front of one picture of James and Eliza at the beach, I squint, trying to imagine what it would be like to be in that photo with them. I've never had a friend so close the two of us would go on vacation together, and I'm excited to have that with Eliza and her family.

Of course, I don't expect them to pay for everything, although I won't turn them down if they offer. I loved going shopping with Eliza and having her foot the bill, and it will be really nice of James to offer to pay my way, but I'm willing to help out as much as I can. I'm a pretty good cook and can easily make all the meals for everyone. Or I'm more than happy to watch the kids while James and Eliza spend time together.

That, or I can stay behind with Knox while the three of them go on vacation. I know Eliza probably won't like that thought at first, but she's the one who's so careful about making sure nobody knows about her son. I'd just be there in the shadows, making sure her wishes are followed exactly.

Although I want to go downstairs and tell Eliza my plan about either taking a vacation with her and James, or staying behind to watch over the kids, now is my chance to show her that I can take care of them, that she doesn't have to worry when I'm in charge.

Taking a deep breath, I walk down the hall to the play-room, only peeking in the master bedroom for a moment. It looks just like I thought it would, with a large four-poster bed, white curtains that match the bedspread, and a fluffy white rug on the floor.

Perfect. Curated. Just like everything in their lives, although I'm the only person in the world to know the truth.

"Hey, guys," I say, poking my head into the playroom before I step in all the way. I debate closing the door behind me so I can make sure we don't bother Eliza while she's working, but decide she'll probably feel better if it's open and she can hear us if there's a problem. Still, I close it halfway, enough to give the three of us a little bit of privacy.

"Hi, Miss Bethany." Penelope's sitting on the floor, an array of stuffed animals around her, all ready for a tea party. She has a plastic teapot in her hands and hesitates for a moment before holding it out to me. "Do you want to pour the tea?"

"I'd be honored." I take it from her and glance at Knox, who's hiding in a fort on the other side of the room. Really, no child needs a playroom this large. It's ridiculous, but the kids seem to love it. "Are you going to join us, Knox?"

"Knox doesn't like tea parties," Penelope says as her brother emphatically shakes his head. "He thinks they're stupid." Her voice drops to a whisper so her brother can't hear her.

"Well, I don't." Gently moving a stuffed bear with only one eye out of the way, I sit down next to Penelope and carefully pour imaginary tea in each of the cups. "Tell me, Penelope, were you excited to be a big sister when Knox came home to live with you?"

She's reaching out to hand a cup of tea to the bear sitting across from her, and she freezes, her eyes flicking over to me before she looks back at the bear.

"I bet it was quite a shock to have him suddenly show up, right? Did you know you were going to be getting a baby brother?"

I'm pushing her. I know I shouldn't, but I can't help myself. It's just not enough for me to know the truth about Knox and what James and Eliza did. I want to know all the gritty details. I want to know if Penelope was aware of the truth, if she was in on the scheme, if she thinks her mom was pregnant, or what lie they told her.

Penelope exhales and finally speaks, not turning to look at me as she does. "It was very exciting," she says, and I can't help but think that she sounds robotic. "I was really happy to be a big sister."

"I bet you were. And you didn't have to deal with a crying baby or anything, did you?" Knox was a toddler when James and Eliza took him.

Penelope shakes her head. "He was a big boy when he became my brother, but I'm not supposed to talk about it."

"Oh, I don't want to get you in trouble," I tell her, picking up a cup and pretending to take a sip of tea. "But your mom and I are good friends, and you know you can tell me anything you want. I won't ever judge you or tell anyone, okay?"

She gives me a stiff nod.

I watch out of the corner of my eye as Knox peers at the two of us from the door of his fort. He's not making any movements to join us, but I can tell he's interested in what's going on out here.

"Are there any other secrets you want to tell me?" I do my best to keep my tone casual, and I don't look at her while I speak. The last thing I want is for Penelope to think she needs to clam up and keep from telling me the truth about anything else Eliza is trying to keep hidden. "Sometimes secrets can feel like big rocks in your stomach until you share them with someone, and then you feel better."

Silence.

"If you want to tell me a secret, I bet I could tell you one first."

This gets her attention. I knew it would. Secrets are currency, and it doesn't matter how old you are, you always want to know when someone else has something hidden that they don't want to share.

The fact that I'm willing to share my secret with her before I ask her to share with me will help make her trust me.

Even though she shouldn't.

"I always wanted a sister growing up," I tell Penelope, taking another sip of my fake tea. "But my parents never had any other kids, so I used to pretend that I had a little sister I could play with all the time. It made me feel better. My secret is that I get envious of other people who have siblings."

Penelope nods, her little face grave. "I wish that when they brought Knox home, he had been a little girl instead of a boy."

"I always wanted a baby. It's sad that some people can't have them."

She looks wise when she nods again, then chews on her lower lip for a moment like what she wants to say to me is something she has to work up the nerve to say. "I heard Mommy and Daddy fighting about Knox."

"Really?" My heart flutters in my chest. Eliza doesn't want to let me in on all of the little secrets in her home. I could help her, could make things better for her and be a good listener, but only if she'll open up to me. The fact that her daughter is willing to do it instead thrills me. "What were they saying?"

"Daddy doesn't think he and Mommy should have brought him home."

So they don't agree on that.

Knowing this makes me feel even closer to Eliza. She did what she believed was right for her family, no matter what her husband thought. It's nice to know that she's willing to do whatever she has to for her kids.

I have to make sure Eliza knows I'm on her side, but that I'm willing to side with James if she does something I don't like.

"Anyway," I tell Penelope, taking another fake sip. "I love that you're sharing with me. What's your favorite type of ice cream? I think I'd like to take you out for some one afternoon."

Her face brightens up. "I love mint chocolate chip," she says, rubbing her stomach. "Yum."

"Would you like to go get ice cream with me someday?" I glance up at her as I speak, hoping to be able to read her face so I can tell exactly what she's thinking.

Without any hesitation, she nods. "I love ice cream, but I don't get to go get it very often, because Knox has to stay in the house. Would it just be you and me?"

"Yep. Just some girl time."

Penelope grins at me, and I smile back. Getting her on my side is an important step in making sure that Eliza can't end our friendship. It's one thing for her to like me, but when her daughter loves spending time with me, then there's no way she can cut me out of her life.

From his fort, Knox stares at me. I'd love for him to come play with the two of us, but it doesn't really matter if he doesn't.

He's a cute little kid, but I have to remember what he really is.

He's blackmail.

32

ELIZA

After reading through the blog post I just wrote one more time and pressing the button to post it, I push back from my desk, my ears straining as I listen for any sound from upstairs.

Bethany's been up there with the kids for a while now, and even though I enjoyed having a little time to myself to write, I don't like thinking about what they may be doing.

But what choice did I have in the matter? It's not like I could have told her she wasn't allowed up there with them. I can only imagine how quickly she would have called the police to turn me in.

Frustrated, I slam my fist down on my desk. James was right: I did this, I brought this all on my family, and now I have to figure out how I'm going to undo it.

Groaning, I push up from my chair and walk out of my office, pausing at the bottom of the stairs to try to hear if there's anything going on in the playroom. It's quiet, too quiet, and the resignation I felt a moment ago over Bethany spending time with my kids disappears as fear takes hold instead.

What the hell am I doing allowing her up there with my kids?
What if she hurts them?
What if she takes them?

The thought of her somehow sneaking my children out the door behind my back when I was working fills me with panic. I can't hear anything but the sound of my heartbeat in my ears as I hurry up the stairs, grabbing the banister and pulling myself up. My palm feels slick with sweat, and I wipe it on my jeans, then keep going.

Still no sound from the playroom as I reach the second floor and turn down the hall.

I can't see the playroom door from here, but I can hear that it's silent.

No.

It was so easy to take Knox, to just pick him up and carry him out of the house while Camilla lay on the bed, drugged and high and unaware of anything going on around her.

Am I just as bad as my sister?

Was I so focused on the article I was writing that Bethany was able to walk by me with the kids, and I didn't hear a thing?

What will the police say when we report not one, but two missing kids, when we try to explain that we have two children, even though there isn't any proof that Knox is ours?

Vomit burns the back of my throat. I take another step, then another, lurching down the hall to the playroom, a scream already on my lips as I push the door all the way open and step inside, my heart beating so hard I feel like I'm going to pass out.

The light's off, the entire room dark. Someone, probably Bethany, has pulled the curtains on the windows, making it even darker in here, making it impossible for me to see anything but vague shapes in the space. I reach for the light switch, feeling more and more like I'm back in Camilla's drug house, the same panic I felt then burning through my body right now.

I hit the switch and then blink hard, the sudden light clicking on overhead temporarily blinding me.

Then I hear a giggle, and I sag backwards, grabbing onto the doorframe for support as all the air rushes out of my body in a long, hard exhale.

Knox pokes his head out from his fort, sees me, giggles, and then pulls his head back into the fort. A moment later, Penelope does the same, gives me a thumbs-up, then disappears again.

"Bethany, I need to talk to you." Even though I'm angry, I try to keep my voice light, try to put a smile on my face so when I do see the woman who's been spending time with my children, I don't look like I want to kill her.

Which I do.

There's some movement in the fort; then Bethany crawls out. Her hair is messed up with static, and she's wearing a half a dozen plastic necklaces I remember buying Penelope for playing dress-up. Crawling on her hands and knees, she clears the fort fully before she stands up, then smiles at me, the expression slowly sliding off her face when she sees the look on mine.

"Eliza, is everything okay?"

"I need to talk to you." Glancing past her at the fort, I'm not surprised that both of my children are now staring at the two of us. "Downstairs. Alone."

"Did I do something wrong?" As if she knows that all hell is going to break loose as soon as I have her away from my kids, she's refusing to move, her feet stuck to the floor like that's going to save her from how upset I am. "We were just playing in the fort."

I thought you were all gone.

"Everything's fine," I tell her, reaching out and lightly taking her by the arm to pull her out of the room. For one horrible moment, I think she's not going to follow me, but then she does, her steps automatic, like she doesn't have a choice in the matter.

"Stay here, kids," I call over my shoulder. "We just need to have an adult conversation, and then you two can come down." I hear Penelope and Knox whispering in the fort, but ignore them as I lead Bethany to the stairs and then gesture for her to walk down them first.

There's no way I want her walking behind me. I don't think that she'd push me, but...

The thought is too horrible; I shake my head to clear it.

We don't speak until we're in the kitchen; then Bethany leans against the counter, her arms crossed, a scowl on her face.

"What? You don't like me spending time with your kids? You don't trust me?"

"It's not that."

"It is. Tell me you don't trust me. Tell me, that you, a *kidnapper*, doesn't trust someone else with your kids. I think you're projecting, Eliza. I thought the two of us were friends."

"But we're not!" The words burst free before I even realize what I'm about to say. Bethany looks angry, and I feel like I should cover it up, should clamp my hands over my mouth— but the words are out in the air between the two of us now, and there isn't a damn thing I can do to take them back.

"You still won't say we're friends?" Bethany asks. She doesn't look surprised; clearly she knows how I still feel. "Because we are. We may not have been at first, but there's no reason for us not to become friends. *Good* friends. Sure, our relationship didn't start out in a traditional way, but you like spending time with me, and so do your kids. We shop together. You had me over for dinner."

"Because I didn't have a choice," I hiss. "Because you were going to blackmail me. You made it more than clear, Bethany, that I have to spend time with you or you're going to tell everyone about Knox. I'm never going to like you, no matter what you might think." I pause, taking a deep breath before continuing, "But there's another way."

She doesn't answer, but I see her eyebrow arch. She's interested.

"I have money," I tell her. "Lots of money. You just let me know how much you want, how much it will cost to keep you out of our lives, and you can have it. I'll give you any amount; you just need to name it."

"You want to pay me off to get me out of your life?"

I knew she'd understand, and I nod. "Yes, that's it. How much will it take to make you go away, to make this all never have happened? I'll pay you whatever you want."

"Why do you think I want money?"

"What?"

She laughs. "Eliza, from day one, the only thing I've wanted is to be your friend. I've made that more than clear time and time again. All you have to do is let me in, let me be your friend. I promise you, I'm loyal. I told you that the two of us are the same, that we're more alike than you ever would admit to yourself... and now you think that I want money, and I'll just go away?"

"Please." I hate begging her, hate the thought that she has the upper hand, but she does, and there isn't anything I can do to change that. Bethany is in complete control, no matter how much I want to pretend that's not true. "Please, just give me an amount. Any amount. I'll pay you whatever you need. I just don't want this."

"You don't want me in your life?"

"I don't want to live in fear that you're going to tell about Knox." There. I'm being honest with her because I don't think I have a choice. She knows she has me backed into a corner, and that there really isn't any way out of this for me. "I don't want this hanging over my head all the time. I'll pay you; you can move; you can live in another country; you can do whatever you want. I'll make it so you don't have to work another day in your life. Just let me have this."

She's silent for a moment. When she does speak, her words have a chill to them. "Let you have what?"

"My kids. My family. My life, without worrying about someone threatening to take it from me."

"But he's not your child."

"He is. I love him." My throat threatens to close up, and I swallow hard, pushing the feeling away. I need to get this woman to see how serious I am, that I'm willing to do whatever it takes to protect my family.

Whatever it takes.

"Then I guess you'll do whatever it takes to keep him safe, won't you?" She stares at me. "You'll be my friend; you'll let me into your perfect little life; you won't try to offer to pay me off again, because that won't keep him safe. Don't push me. You think that you're the better person because you have money, but I'm the person with all the control here. Don't forget that."

Spinning away from me, she stalks out of the kitchen, headed back for the stairs. I watch her go, unable to get my feet to work to follow her.

My mind keeps turning over and over what she just said.

She knows I'll do whatever it takes to keep Knox safe, to protect my family, to ensure that nobody can ever hurt us. She's too stupid to take the money and run, which means that I'm now backed into a corner.

But that doesn't mean I'm going to stop fighting.

She wants to be friends? We're not friends.

She wants to put my family in danger? I'm not going to let that happen.

I'm going to kill Bethany.

33

BETHANY

It was obvious Eliza wanted me to leave before lunch, but I had nothing to do today, so I ate sandwiches with her and her two kids, then suggested that Penelope, Knox, and I watch a movie. It wasn't easy to ignore the way Eliza was glaring at me.

She still doesn't get it. We've talked about it, over and over, and while we didn't start out as friends, that doesn't mean we're not going to be friends.

It wasn't like this at first. I was so hopeful this would be easy. Sure, friendships can have growing pains, but she hurt me today. When she told me that our friendship wasn't ever going to happen and then offered to pay me off, I just...

Something changed. She doesn't want to be friends? I'm not fine with that. I want her in my life. I want her to go shopping with me, to want to celebrate with me. I'm angry with her, but I think I can still get what I want.

I can still make her my friend.

She can get angry all she wants, but I'm not going to just walk away. It really offended me that she had the gall to offer to pay me to go away. I'm not going away; that's what she needs to get through her head.

I'm here to stay. There's nothing she can do about it.

That's why, even though I know she's antsy to get me to leave the house before James gets home, and even though I'm going to be pushing it to get to work on time, I'm still sitting in her living room, Penelope next to me on the sofa, reading her a book.

I always loved Dr. Seuss, always loved his silly little rhymes and cute drawings, and Penelope enjoys it just as much as I do. Even Knox is listening, though he's sitting on a chair on the other side of the coffee table, like he's not sure if he wants to get any closer to the two of us.

Eliza, for her part, keeps hovering in the doorway. She's doing everything she can to get me to leave, but I'm not going until I'm ready. That won't be until I get to see James and he can learn that I was here with his family all day long, taking care of them and playing with the kids.

The sound of the garage door closing makes Penelope sit straight up, and even though we still have a few pages left in *One Fish, Two Fish, Red Fish, Blue Fish,* she darts away from me, Knox right on her heels.

It gives Eliza the chance she's been waiting for. I don't have time to get off the sofa before she's standing right in front of me, leaning down a bit so she can talk to me.

"I don't know what you're planning, Bethany, but you need to know that it's not going to work."

Blinking up at her, I wonder how to make her see what I really want. "I just want to be your friend. I want to be involved with the kids. I don't want your money, Eliza."

"You can't be around them." She hisses the words at me, but keeps her voice quiet so nobody will be able to hear her. What she's saying is for my ears alone.

I stare at her. I thought, when I found her online and

started meeting up with her, that her heart and soul would be as gorgeous as the posts she makes online, but I had no idea how wrong I was. I had no idea that she would hiss at me like this, that she wouldn't let me spend time with the kids, even though I'm doing everything I can to prove that I won't hurt them.

I just wanted to be her friend.

"You really want to push me?" Standing up, I force her to take a step back from me. I'm breathing hard, but so is she, both of us sounding like we just ran a marathon. "Seriously, Eliza, is this what you want to do? I could *ruin you.*"

"You wouldn't."

I'm angry, and I know I need to watch what I say, but she's been rude to me all day. I'm ready to let it all out. The words tumble free before I can stop them.

"I would. I know your secret, Eliza. All I wanted was to be your friend, and I'm not sure why you won't let me do that. That's all I wanted, yet you have to push me away. Your kids like me. Penelope—"

"You need to stay away from my kids."

I open my mouth to respond, to remind her that she doesn't really have any say in the matter, and that she'd better be kinder to me, to her *friend*, if she doesn't want to lose everything, when James walks into the living room.

The tension between the two of us, which was so thick it was choking, dissipates a little bit as he walks over to us.

"Is everything okay?" He sounds nervous, and his eyes flick back and forth between his wife and me. "Eliza?" When he reaches out and lightly puts his hand on her shoulder, she finally starts, then blinks, like she's coming out of a fugue state.

"Everything's fine," she says, but her voice is tight. "Bethany spent the afternoon here and played with the kids."

"I've been here since the morning," I correct. "The kids

and I played while Eliza got some work done; then we all had lunch and hung out. It was a great day." I grin at James.

He doesn't return it.

"Well, I'm sure Eliza really appreciates getting to have some time to herself to write her blog," he says slowly, then finally smiles at me. "Thank you for coming over; it was obviously a great day."

"We should do it again soon." I turn to Eliza, who's staring at her husband. "Tomorrow? Or how about Wednesday? Why don't you and I have another Target shopping trip?"

"Wednesday sounds great." Eliza finally turns to look at me. "I'll meet you at Target."

"No, I'll pick you up. And who knows, Eliza, maybe I'll take some time to think more about what you offered. Why don't you talk to James and see how much you two are willing to spend?"

I walk away, looking for the kids to say goodbye. Something about the way Eliza offered me money earlier today makes me think she and James didn't talk about it. It's not that I want her to get in trouble with her husband, but I don't mind the thought of the two of them talking about me.

I have the two of them right where I want them. If I play my cards right, then tonight will be my last night waiting tables.

I'm thrilled with the guest room in this house, which is great.

Because soon, it's going to be mine.

34

ELIZA

I know I should go to the front door and make sure Bethany leaves, but right now, I feel stuck in place by James; all I can do is listen to her say goodbye to the kids before letting herself out and quietly shutting the door.

It feels like someone just rolled a rock across the exit of my tomb.

James is staring at me, the look on his face impossible for me to read. I do my best to ignore him for a moment, but I know I need to tell him what just happened. I know what he's going to ask, what he's going to want me to do, and even though I know that killing Bethany is the best way to get rid of my little problem, I'm not sure I can do it.

"What was she talking about, Eliza? How much are you willing to spend on what?"

A shiver runs through me when I look up at my husband, making myself meet his eyes. "How much we'd be willing to pay her to get her to go away."

"What?" He frowns, then scrubs his hand down his face. "You've got to be kidding. You offered her money?"

"To leave us alone, yes! I thought she'd be greedy and

she'd take it, that we could get her to back off without having to do something drastic." My voice drops on the last word as I imagine what our kids would think if they were to overhear what the two of us are talking about.

He pauses. "And what did she say?"

"She said no. But then she brought it up when she was leaving, so maybe... maybe she'd take some?"

I'm hopeful, even though I'm not convinced this is going to work out in our favor. I have to hope that it will, because I can't let this woman around my children again. It's just not safe.

"Do you think she would? She might go away." He pauses, then continues, "It might be worth it to pay her off. It's better than—"

"Killing her," I agree.

He exhales, and we stand in silence for a moment, both of us lost in our thoughts.

"Okay. Here's the plan," he says. "We're going to have a nice dinner here with the kids and pretend like none of this happened. I want you to think about an amount you'd be comfortable giving her to make her go away, and I'll do the same. When the kids are in bed, we'll talk about it. I know we don't keep high balances in our savings accounts, but there's plenty in retirement and investments, and we could always sell some stock if we need to."

"Right, good plan." I exhale shakily, trying to convince myself that James and I can get through this. We've always gotten through everything we've faced, no matter what it was. Even when I was convinced the police were going to come for us after we took Knox, he was there for me; he talked me down off the ledge.

This is just one more time I get to see how much my husband loves me. We're a team, even though I know a lot of the blame rests on my shoulders. I know he blames me for what's happening—he's said as much. Running my blog and posting so many pictures of our family while we had Knox was stupid, but I couldn't help myself.

Now I wish I'd never started blogging. I wish I'd never even thought about a social media account. We could still have Knox, could still have our little family, but Bethany wouldn't be a problem.

"I know we talked about killing her, but this has to be a better option," I say, and James nods, wrapping his arms around me and pulling me to his chest for a hug. For a moment, I let myself rest there, enjoying the steady beat of his heart, how he smells after a long day at work.

It's nice to have him comfort me, to feel like we're on the same page, in this together. He knows I'd do anything for the kids, and for a while there, I felt like he was pushing me to handle Bethany on my own.

And it's true, I can do anything I put my mind to... but I want James with me.

"We're going to end this," he promises me. "Okay? But first, I want to see our kids and eat something delicious. Then we'll all play a board game and get them in bed. No more thinking about Bethany until the kids are in their pjs and passed out, okay?"

"Deal." Going up on my tiptoes, I kiss him, then pull away from his hug so I can call the kids to come help me set the table. "Penelope, Knox, it's time for dinner! Meet me in the kitchen!"

Nothing. No groaning, no laughing, no pattering of little feet as the two of them race each other down the hall to the kitchen.

James and I stand completely still.

"Penelope? Knox?"

The same fear I felt earlier when walking up the stairs, convinced that something bad had happened to them, washes over me again. I place a hand on James' chest for support as I try to keep my knees from giving out.

"Where are they?" He sounds interested, but not yet concerned. He doesn't know about the fear I had of losing them earlier today. He doesn't know how terrified I was when I thought Bethany had done something to them.

She hadn't.

That time.

35

ELIZA

"**K**nox! Penelope!" I'm screaming my kids' names, and I push away from James, running out the door to the hall, my eyes scanning the space as I try to remember all of their newest favorite hiding spots.

In the front closet.

Under the kitchen table.

Next to the sofa, squeezed in by the bookshelf that's stuffed full of books I don't have time to read anymore.

James is hot on my heels as I look in each of the places, the panic I feel squeezing my chest growing with every second that I don't find our kids.

"She took them!" Whirling around to face him, I plant my hands on his shoulders and shove him back a bit. I know I shouldn't be mad at him, that he didn't do anything wrong, but I want to make him feel as scared as I do. I want him to ache for my babies and help me bring them home.

"She wouldn't," he says, but he doesn't sound confident. "Eliza, she knows we'd call the police if she did something like that, and then she'd have a lot of explaining to do."

"No." I moan the word, shaking my head. "If she left Knox

behind, then I would call the police because we could explain Penelope, but not him. But she didn't leave him. She took him. He's collateral. *Blackmail.* He's what's going to keep us from murdering her. She has to know, has to have figured out that we're not going to let her ruin our lives anymore."

"Stop it." Stepping back from me, he lets my hands fall from his shoulders, then stares down at me like he doesn't recognize me. "Stop it, Eliza. *You* let her into the house. *You* let her spend time with the kids. Now what the hell are we going to do?"

I don't know. I honestly have no idea what to do, how to bring the kids back. They're not in the house, that much is sure. They would have come when I called, or we would have found them, but the fact that they're still gone...

James shakes his head and steps to the side. I look past him, my eyes falling on the front door.

It's not locked.

"Outside?" I push past my husband, my hand already extended as I reach the door. For a moment, I feel like my fingers aren't going to work. Then they close on the door-knob, and I twist it hard, opening the door.

Cool air rushes into the house; then I'm on the porch, James right behind me. The kids aren't in the rocking chairs right by the front door. They're not picking flowers from the planters, and they're not kicking a ball around on the porch —but then someone laughs. I grab the porch railing, holding onto it to keep from falling over.

"Knox, no!" It's Penelope, her voice floating around the side of the house to us.

James takes off before I realize what just happened, what the sound of Penelope calling her brother really means for us.

He's outside. In the front yard.
Where someone can see him.

James is already down the steps that lead from the porch to the walkway, and I hurry after him, fear coursing through my body.

Someone will see Knox. Someone is going to hear Penelope calling him, and look out the window. They're going to see him, and then everything James and I have tried to do to keep him safe is all going to fall apart.

And it's Bethany's fault.

James reaches the kids first, and he scoops Knox up into his arms, holding him close like he's injured, before turning and running past me back into the house. Penelope stops running, her mouth falling open, her eyes welling up with tears when I reach her.

Dropping to my knees in front of her, I take her by the shoulders, forcing her to look at me. "Are you okay? Why are you out here? Why did Knox come with you?" My questions are coming too fast, and she blinks at me, tears now streaming down her face.

"I'm sorry!" She tries to pull away from me, like she's going to chase James up to the house, but I can't seem to let her go.

"Why did he come out here?" Yelling at her isn't going to help. Screaming in her face isn't going to let Penelope calm down enough to answer my question, but I can't stop myself. I'm terrified of what Knox being out here might mean for our family.

"She said to come out and wave to her!" Penelope twists away from me, taking a step back and staring at me like she hates me. "She said she'd like it if we waved, and so we did, and then Knox started running around the yard, and I chased after him to stop him!"

She's breathing hard, both of us sucking air. "Bethany told you to come out here and wave to her?"

She nods, reaching up with clenched fists to wipe the tears from her cheeks.

"And that's why you were out here?"

Another nod.

Bethany knew.

She knew that my kids would follow her outside after having such a great day with her, one where they didn't realize I was beyond stressed at the idea of something terrible happening to them. More than that, though, she knew that having Knox come outside would put him in danger of someone seeing him.

And she did it anyway.

Taking Penelope by the hand, I guide her to the house. I'm smiling, just so she doesn't get scared of the look on my face, but on the inside, I'm seething.

Forget paying her off.

This has to end.

36

BETHANY

I'm tying my apron around my waist, making sure that it's nice and tight so that it doesn't slip off while I'm working, when Cindy pokes her head into the back to speak to me, her eyes wide.

She looks like she's thrilled with whatever she's going to say, like she's been waiting for years to get involved in any drama like this, and I freeze, already sure that I know what's going on.

"Someone is here to see you, and they're pissed." Her eyes flick up and down my body, like she's taking me in for the last time before I disappear. "Told me that I need to find you, get you out there, and that they weren't going to take no for an answer."

I don't want to go out there, because I'm sure what's going to happen as soon as I do. Eliza wasn't ever going to let it fly that I spent all day at her house and then convinced the kids to come outside to wave goodbye to me. But she needed to see that I'm in control here, not her. I need her to see that she has to be my friend.

"Are they causing a scene?" My fingers flutter at the front of my apron where I just tied the bow nice and tight.

Cindy nods. "He's on the verge of yelling."

He?

I honestly expected Eliza to be the one standing in the bar, waiting for me to come out so she could scream at me. But if it's James, if he's the one who came to see me, then things are definitely not shaking out the way I thought they would. I don't know him as well as Eliza, so I'm not sure how he's going to handle everything that's been going on.

But from what Cindy's saying, I also don't have much of a choice in finding out. If he stands out there in the bar and continues to cause a scene, then the chances are good that I'm going to get fired, and I can't let that happen until I know I have another job lined up.

Like being a live-in nanny for Penelope and Knox.

A wave of frustration washes over me when I think about the fact that I probably blew it by the way I acted at the house. Even if Eliza had been on the fence about having me move in with her family to look out for the kids, I probably lost that opportunity when I had the two of them come outside to wave goodbye to me without permission from their mom.

And yes, I knew what I was doing.

I always do.

Putting my best contrite face on, I push past Cindy, well aware that she's going to follow me out into the bar so she can see how this is all going to play out. Any drama at work is something we all live for, especially when it doesn't involve us. None of us want to be at the center of the problem, but we all want to watch when someone else is.

Sure enough, it's James standing by the bar, his back to me. He has his hands planted on the wooden surface and an empty shot glass in front of him. Even as I walk up, I can

smell the alcohol on him, and I'm pretty sure he didn't get
that drunk in our bar. The bartender gives me a glance, like
he's really sorry for what I'm about to face, but before I can
return his smile, James turns, his eyes darkening when he
sees me.

"Bethany."

"I can explain," I say, holding my hands up between the
two of us. "Really, I can. I'm so sorry, James, I acted without
thinking."

He cuts me off when I take a breath, obviously not interested in whatever else I'm going to say. "You could have
ruined everything."

Heat flames in my face. Everyone is watching me, even
the patrons sitting around the room drinking. I can just hear
what they're thinking: *This is so much better than staying in and
watching reruns. Who knew going to the bar could be so enter-
taining?*

"But I didn't. The kids are fine." The last thing I want is
for all of my co-workers and the patrons to know what
happened, so I drop my voice as I reach James. "Please, let's
go outside or to the back or something, and we can talk about
this. I don't want to make a scene at my job."

I don't want to lose my job.

"You need to leave us alone." He doesn't budge from his
spot by the bar. "You need to disappear from our lives,
pretend we never met, stop stalking my wife and leave my
family alone. You almost ruined everything; do you understand that? We'll pay you if that's what it takes. Just... leave us
alone."

"I understand." I'm mollified, but mostly because I hate
the way everyone is staring at the two of us. If he would just
join me outside, then the two of us could talk this over. The
fact that he's so hell-bent on airing our dirty laundry where
everyone can see it pisses me off.

It also pisses me off that James and Eliza are still harping on about the money. I clear my throat. "I don't want your money," I begin, but he cuts me off.

"Then never come by the house again. Never contact Eliza; stop following her on social media. This is over, Bethany. Don't make me call the cops."

Oh, there it is. The self-righteous bullshit I had a very good feeling he was going to pull. James and Eliza act like they're the victims here, like they haven't done anything wrong. They like to pretend like I'm coming into their lives just to screw up their perfect family when they know full well that their family isn't perfect.

"Fine." It kills me to spit the word at him, but I do it anyway, because I'm more interested in getting him to leave me alone than anything else. I need time to think about this, to figure out how I'm going to salvage my friendship with Eliza.

The fact that she sent her husband to come talk to me and didn't want to do it herself upsets me, but I don't want to show him that.

Or did he get drunk and come without her permission?

I can see that. I can see him storming out of the house to try to take care of this on his own. I can also imagine her sitting at home, her kids next to her on the sofa, typing away on a blog post about how important it is to be a great friend when someone needs you while her husband screams at me in the bar.

That's all I wanted from her—for her to be a great friend. She has everything, the perfect life, the perfect family, the adoring readers who want to know every little detail of her life, and the moment she has someone to share all of that with, she throws me away.

"Good. I'm glad you understand. Come by again, and

we'll call the police." He starts to walk away from me, but I reach out, grabbing his arm and pulling him back.

James stops walking, and from this close to him, I can smell a faint trace of his cologne. His skin feels warm, even through his long-sleeve shirt. I have a very good feeling he's sweating as he waits for me to speak.

"I want you to remember, James, that if you call the police, I'll make sure I'm not the only one walking out of that house in handcuffs." I pause, and when he doesn't respond, I continue, "How do you think little Knox and Penelope would feel watching you get led away and put in the back of a cop car?"

Instead of responding, he wrenches his arm out of my grasp and then storms across the bar without looking back. There's still no movement in the room; everyone is watching the two of us. They all want to know what's going to happen next.

So do I.

It's one thing for Eliza to try to pay me off to get me to stop being her friend. That hurt more than I want to admit, but to threaten to call the police if I were to show up at their house again?

I don't think I can let that slide.

Eliza thinks she has all the power right now. I can just imagine James whispering in her ear, telling her that she's right, that the two of them are in complete control.

But they don't have all the power.

I do.

I'm the one who can ruin everything, not them.

My hands clench into fists as I watch the door swing shut behind him. The room is still silent, but right now, I don't care that everyone is staring at me. I'm going to handle this. I don't want to hurt her, don't want to hurt her kids. Eliza is so important to me that I think I can overlook what just happened here, but she needs to know I'm in control. She needs to know this friendship isn't optional.

I'll give her one more chance, because that's the type of friend I am.

But if she pushes me away again, I'm going to make sure everyone in the world knows what type of person she really is.

37

ELIZA

"How did she handle it?"

I'm nervous as I watch James walk back and forth in front of the living room sofa, his hands clasped tightly behind his back, his brow furrowed.

I was ready to go to her job and tell her off. I was ready to call the police and report her for... for what, I wasn't sure. Stalking? Harassment? She'd tell them that I opened the front door for her and invited her in, and while it wasn't the entire truth, it was true enough that I don't think the police would have believed me.

Instead of helping me fix anything, what did James do? Get me to tell him where she worked, then drove off in a fit of rage. I cried, calling him over and over and begging him not to go, but he wasn't listening to any of it.

He likes to fix things, and he thought for sure this was one thing he could take care of on his own, especially after he pounded back the whiskey before walking out the door.

I can't believe that she didn't call the police, but there aren't any cops in the driveway. Still, I'm terrified of what he might have done, what he might push her to do.

What if she tells the truth about Knox?

Anger floods through me when I think about the fact that she has so much control. It's not fair, not right that she should be able to have any control over me, over the situation, but she has me by the balls, as James would say.

"She's going to back off," James tells me, but I shake my head before he's even finished speaking.

"She won't."

He stops pacing and stares at me. "Why do you say that?"

"Because I know her. Because she's insane. Because she has leverage over me, and there's no way she's going to give that up, not if she thinks she can get away with hurting me."

"She seemed pretty scared when I was at her job."

"Probably because she doesn't want to lose it." I pause, thinking. "Did you offer her money again? Maybe make her see that her best option really is to take the money and run?" I really don't think she'll take it, but I still have a glimmer of hope.

It's quickly squashed with his answer. "She won't take the money."

"So why the hell did you go? Just to be drunk and yell at her? You shouldn't have done that. If either of us was going to go, I should have gone, not you—not drunk, not when we're talking about killing her. Not that it would have made a difference." I'm gasping for air, and he walks over to hug me, but I jerk away from him and drop down on the sofa. "Dammit, James, you should have stayed here so we could figure it out together, not create a bunch of witnesses who know you two got in a fight!"

He hates it when I yell, and I know it scares the kids when they hear it, but they're both in bed. James stares at me like he can't believe I'd raise my voice like this to him. Even though I know I should feel bad, I don't.

"You would have killed her if you'd gone. I wanted to see

if there was another way. I just needed to know." James walks over to me and sits next to me on the sofa. I resist the urge to lean into him and let him swing his arm around my shoulders. "You know you would have, Eliza. Or even if you didn't kill her, you would have done something we would regret. I couldn't let you go. The kids needed you here."

"Something we would regret, like going to confront her at her job?" I hiss the words at him, but he doesn't answer. "Maybe she needs to die. You said it yourself, James, and I was scared, but now I'm not. We need to kill Bethany. I don't know how we're going to do it, but we have to stop her, have to get rid of her. It's the only way we're going to be able to keep our secret and not end up in jail. And who would stop us? She's pathetic; she has no friends, hardly any followers on social media. Why shouldn't we just handle this?"

When James doesn't immediately say anything, I turn to look at him. He sucks in a breath and gives his head a little shake.

"Why not?" I feel frustration bubble up in me at the fact that my husband would mention this idea himself, but now that I'm on board, he's no longer keen on it. Sure, I'd thought about killing Bethany, but for him to suggest it, to mention it as a real option, that pushed it over the edge into the realm of possibility. "You're the one who came up with the idea in the first place. Why would you want to back out now? That's not fair to me, James, and you know it."

"I said it in anger. I said it because I didn't know what else to do. But we can't kill her, Eliza, not really. How the hell do you think you'd cover that up? We weren't even able to keep Knox a secret."

He's pointing his finger at me and blaming me for Bethany finding out about Knox. Even though it makes me angry to think he'd turn on me like this, I ignore it.

I need to stay calm. I need to keep him on the right track,

make sure he knows I'm not going to back down until I know my family is safe. Maybe James wants to leave things up to chance, but I don't. That's why I knew, the first time we saw Knox, that we needed to save him. This is no different. He needs someone to save him, as does Penelope. Our family needs saving, and I'm willing to do whatever I have to.

"It's not like I'm going to write a blog about how to kill your stalker and keep it secret." I smile at him, hoping to thaw the ice around us a little bit, but he doesn't smile back. "We'll be careful. Come on, James, you must have thought about it too, or you wouldn't have suggested it that first time. Don't pretend like the thought hasn't really crossed your mind."

"Of course it has," he snaps. "You don't think I know how much easier our lives would be if she were just gone?" He snaps his fingers by my face, and I wince. "But that doesn't mean we can do it."

"Yes, we can." I take his hand, looping our fingers together. It isn't fair that I have to be the one to convince him of what we need to do, not when he suggested it first. He's supposed to be the strong one, the one willing to do whatever it takes to protect our family.

I think he's still that man. He's just scared, but I'll be with him every step of the way.

I need him to be that man. That, or I need him to get out of the way so I can protect my kids.

"We need to kill her," I say, squeezing his hand. "We need to stop her from hurting our family, from taking us from our kids. We'll never see them again, James, if she gets her way. Are you willing to let that happen?"

"I'm just not sure how to do it." He sounds defeated, and I lean my head against his shoulder, relieved. It's terrible to be this happy that my husband is bending to my will and to what I think needs to be done, but the fact that he's already coming around to my way of thinking means this should be a lot easier than I thought a minute ago.

"I'm sure you have access to drugs we can use." I try to keep my voice light so he doesn't get scared. "James, all you have to do is get your hands on them, bring them home, and I'll take care of the rest. I'll let Bethany know that tonight was a mistake, that I still want to be friends with her, that calling off our friendship was a mistake. Can you think of any drugs that will work?"

A slow nod, but it's still a nod, and it tells me that my husband is still on board with me.

A flash of triumph shoots through me.

"Bring them home tomorrow," I tell him, "and I'll take care of everything. I'll make sure she eats them, or I'll inject her, or whatever it is that I have to do, but all you have to do is get them for me. Can you do that?"

"I can do that. But what will you do with her body? It's not like we can just leave her in our living room. We can't call the paramedics and act like she just up and died, right here at our house, without people getting suspicious."

"I've always wanted to redo our garden," I tell him. "Now might be the time."

The thought of Bethany out in the backyard, her body decomposing right under my flower beds, should make me shiver; it should fill me with dread.

But it doesn't.

It excites me. If I do this right, I can end this.

I have to, for my family.

38

BETHANY

From the moment Cindy told me that a customer was in the bar, yelling and demanding to talk to me, I knew I was going to lose my job, and I was right.

Ripping my apron off, I throw it on the floor, not caring if it gets filthy, because it's not like I'm ever going to wear it again. All that matters to me right now is getting out of here as quickly as possible, hiding my face from Cindy and my other co-workers, and never showing back up here again.

Well, that is, until I need my last paycheck.

If my boss would just get with the times and set up direct deposit, then I'd be able to walk away from this place and never look back. Taking a deep breath, I grab my purse, sling it over my shoulder, and turn to walk out of here for the second-to-last time ever, when Cindy pops through the door, stopping right in front of me.

"Cindy, I just want to go home," I say, trying to sidestep her, but she doesn't let me pass.

"You have to tell me what that was all about." She's starving for the drama, and while I normally would love to gossip with her over what was going on with our patrons, it's different to be the one being gossiped about. I don't like it.

"I don't have to tell you anything."

"You were having an affair with him, weren't you?" She stares at me, then takes in my entire body like she's trying to judge for herself whether or not someone would stoop to having an affair with me. "I saw the way he looked at you when you walked out there, like he couldn't get enough of you."

"Hardly." Now I'm frustrated, because the one thing I didn't want out of this was James. All I really wanted was Eliza's friendship. The thought that people will think it ended because I was stupid enough to have an affair with a married man is infuriating.

"You can tell me." Cindy's so close to me right now that I can smell her peppermint gum. She's breathing right in my face, her breath warm on my cheek, but I shake her off.

Telling her would be stupid. It's my secret, my blackmail to hold over Eliza and James. Letting anyone else in on the secret will only dilute it, will only result in me no longer being in control. I know Cindy would love nothing more than to learn the truth about what happened with James that he would come here to yell at me like this, but I can't tell her.

Right?

"I just want to go home," I say, finally getting past her. "I'll be by later this week to pick up my check, okay?"

"I'll be waiting." She looks disappointed, but still manages to put a smile on her face when I turn around to look at her. "Seriously, though, Bethany, I know you don't have a lot of friends. There's no reason why I can't be that person for you."

"I have a best friend," I say stiffly. "Eliza. She'll be there for me."

The words are automatic. Even though I know Eliza won't

be there for me, not right now, not when she blames every-thing on me, I don't want Cindy to think I want her sympathy. I don't need her pity friendship. Even though the two of us work together, we aren't anything alike.

Eliza and I are the same. That's what I've been trying to make her understand.

"Still, I want to know!" Cindy calls after me as I let the door close behind me. Once out in the main bar, I notice how everyone grows silent and glances at me. They're just like Cindy, all of them wanting to know what's happening.

I could tell them.

When I throw open the door to the sidewalk, I take a deep breath, the cool night air filling my lungs.

She offered me money, but I turned her down.

I offered her friendship, but she turned me away.

I could take it all from her, and I want to. Right now, I want nothing more than to go to the police and tell them about Knox. I want to watch as her perfect little life is ripped away from her, but I don't want to do that to her kids, and I certainly don't want to do that to myself.

Eliza is my ticket out of here. If I turn her over to the police, then I'm effectively shooting myself in the foot.

"There has to be a way the two of us can both get what we want," I mutter, turning in the direction of my apartment. My lease is about to run out, because I thought by now Eliza would have invited me to move in with her. But it looks like I have to spend at least a few more nights in my own place.

Even though I know it's insane to forgive her for what she's done to me, I do. Eliza's scared, and I get that. I've been scared before, been in a position where I don't know whom I can trust. But she doesn't have to be alone.

I'll give her a day or two to cool off; then I'm going to go see her again. Once she's had some time to get her head on straight and realize that having me in her life is really the best option for all of us, I'm sure she'll be more willing to sit down and listen to what I have to say.

And if she's not, then she loses it all.

Mutual self-destruction.

But the thing is, Eliza has a hell of a lot more to lose than I do.

39

ELIZA

It's been two days since I've heard from Bethany, two days since James went to see her at work, two days in which my nerves have felt completely frazzled and I've had to do my best to keep from coming completely unhinged.

If my family notices that I'm so on edge, they don't say anything. I try to act like nothing's wrong, like I'm as happy as I've ever been, but my thoughts of the woman who threatened to ruin my life aren't kind.

If I happened to see her walking on the sidewalk when I was driving somewhere, and she didn't move out of the way, when I zipped by her...

I might not zip on by.

The thought of hurting her the way she's threatened to hurt my family has become all I can think about. The only thing I can do is focus on her, check my phone for messages from her, and stalk her Instagram as relentlessly as she stalked mine.

I'm checking out her newest post, one with a bullshit caption about how the things in life that no longer serve us will disappear from our lives without any pain, when a text pops up from her. My heart skips a beat.

One last chance.

Or what?

Or she'll turn me in. Or she'll tell the police the truth about Knox. The thought sits heavy in my stomach, like a rock, and even though I want to believe that she wouldn't do this to me, she's unhinged. Crazy. Of course she would.

Bethany would do whatever it takes to get what she really wants.

I ignore her text, then lean over to look out the window. Penelope's in the front yard playing on the sidewalk while Knox naps. I hadn't wanted to let her go out there. In fact, the thought of her being anywhere where Bethany could get to her terrified me, but she'd fussed and carried on, and finally I relented, telling her she could play outside as long as she stayed where I could see her, and as long as she ran inside at the first sign of a car.

It's stupid, what I'm about to do, but I can't help it. I need to end this with Bethany, need to be able to sleep at night without worrying about her hurting my family.

"Come here after dinner," I say as I type out the words. "We can talk about it then." My fingers shake, but she'll never be able to tell how nervous I am through the text.

She'll come tonight, when the kids are in bed, and James and I will end this. We'll kill her, bury her in the backyard, and I won't ever have to worry about her coming for us again.

Five minutes go by before she responds. I'm afraid at first she's not going to agree to come over, but my phone finally chimes, and I gasp, grabbing it and flipping it over.

I'll be there.

Good. There's no need to respond to that. The only thing that matters is knowing that she'll come, we'll be able to kill her, and I won't ever have to worry about her threatening my family again.

It's horrible to think about killing someone, but she brought this on herself. I didn't do it to her.

Bethany did it to herself. I'm sure she'd never understand that this is something she pushed me to do, which is why I can't ever try to explain it to her.

The slam of the front door pulls me from my thoughts. Penelope is suddenly in front of me, her sidewalk chalk abandoned on the front walk, her eyes wide.

"A car." She gasps out the words, and I fly from my seat, running to the front door to throw the lock before I peek out the window.

It's a mail truck, late on its route, and I watch as it drives by the house, my body tucked behind the door so they won't be able to see me.

"It's just the mail," I say to my daughter, then hug her to me. "You know what, Daddy will be home soon. Why don't you stay inside and help me make dinner? We need to get Knox up from his nap, or he'll never sleep tonight, and then the four of us can have a nice quiet night."

And I'll finally get rid of Bethany.

A few hours later, after dinner, the kids are in their rooms, and James and I are in the kitchen, both of us sitting at the table. He's spinning his wedding ring around on his finger, something he only does when he's nervous. Between us, on the table, sits a small white box with a syringe inside.

"All we have to do is inject her with it," he tells me,

reaching out and lightly touching the box. "It'll knock her out, and we'll be able to..." His voice fades off.

"Kill her," I offer, making sure my voice sounds as strong as I want it to be.

He nods, swallowing hard. "Right. I can start digging the hole then, but I didn't want the kids to see anything. I don't want them asking any questions."

"They won't. She's nothing to them, and from what you said about where she worked, she's nothing to everyone she meets. This is the best option we have, James." I take his hand in mine and squeeze it until he finally looks at me.

His face is drawn. Pale. Regret that I pushed him to this makes me feel sick, but I can't focus on that right now.

"You're really fine with killing her? You know you can't come back from this—neither of us can. To kill someone, to take their life, that's the biggest thing in the world."

A squeak above our heads makes us both pause and look up at the ceiling. There's no way the kids are out of bed. They were both exhausted when we tucked them in.

That's the problem with old houses. They have noises that can be creepy.

"I would kill anyone who tried to hurt my family," I tell him. My voice is louder than it probably needs to be, but I don't want to hold back right now. It's important I prove to James just what I'm willing to do for the four of us. "I swear to you, James, I'll kill anyone who even thinks about trying to hurt my family. It's not an option to me."

"Killing someone. Dammit." He lets go of my hand and stands up.

There's another squeak from upstairs. I look back up at the ceiling, wondering if I should go check on that noise, but I don't.

There are too many things to do before our guest gets here, and we can finally take care of her.

Nothing else matters.

40

BETHANY

Eliza thinks I'm stupid, but I'm not.

I know a trap when I see one, and there's no way I believe for one second that she and James want to have me over just to talk. He wouldn't have come to my bar and made such a scene if that were the case.

I don't know if I'm ever going to be able to get over the rage I feel when I remember how it felt to have him come to my job and freak out on me like that. Even though I didn't love working there, even though I always knew it wasn't going to be a forever thing, it still pisses me off that the reason I got fired was because of him.

All I've ever done is tried to be a good friend to his wife.

I'm early getting to Eliza's house, and I circle the block, driving slowly before I pull over to the curb a few houses from theirs. They're probably going to be looking out the window for me, waiting for me to arrive in their driveway, so that's the reason I don't want to park right in front of their house.

It's one thing to come here when the little voice in the back of my head is screaming at me that it's a trap, but it's another entirely to drive right up to their house and park where they can see me and I can't see them.

Maybe this is stupid. Part of me hopes against hope that they're going to open their home to me, that whatever bad blood there was between all of us will be gone, and that they're going to have changed their minds about wanting me in their lives.

As much as I hope that is the case, I'm not stupid. I'm not naive.

They didn't call me here because they suddenly want to be friends.

I sit in my car, my heart pounding, my eyes locked on their front door. Even though I know I need to get out of the car and go up to their house, I'm here early for a reason, and that's so I can keep an eye on things. The upstairs lights in the house are all off, which clues me in to the fact that the kids are asleep.

Downstairs, though, the entire place is lit up like the Fourth of July. Even with curtains over the windows, light streams out through the fabric, making the entire house seem to glow.

Eliza and James pass in front of the windows in the living room, and I stiffen as I watch them. Even though it's hard to make out their shapes, and I can't hear what they're saying, I have a feeling they're arguing.

It's just something about their body language, about the way the two of them are standing apart, facing each other, but neither of them is moving to touch the other one. I'd do anything to know what's being said in that house.

Finally I get out of my car, shutting my door as quietly as possible behind me. The two figures in the window don't move, and I keep my eyes on them as I walk up the sidewalk, then cross the street to their house.

That's when the front door opens. I freeze, then step

behind a tree in their front yard, not wanting anyone to see me. From my vantage point, I can see the window where the Sullivans are backlit by the light, as well as the front door.

Someone else is coming out.

It takes a moment, but then Penelope walks out, her little brother in front of her. I can see how she has his hands on his back, pushing him out the door before her before stopping and turning to pull the door shut.

The two figures in the window don't move.

Either they're too busy arguing to notice that their kids are gone, or they just don't care. No way do I think that Eliza would be okay with her children outside after dark like this, especially Knox, so that tells me the argument between her and her husband is so intense that neither of them are paying attention to what's going on in their house.

There's the sound of a soft voice; then Penelope and Knox are down off the porch, moving along the walkway toward the sidewalk.

Toward me.

"Hey," I whisper, stepping out from behind the tree. My hands are up in front of my body, so the kids can see I'm not a threat, even though I'm half-terrified that one of them is going to scream and give me away. "Hey, what are you two doing?"

Penelope stiffens, then looks back at the house. From here, she can see her parents in the window, just like I can.

I'm on pins and needles, waiting for her to do something stupid, waiting for her to make a run back to the house. I'll stop her. I'll chase her down, keep her from reaching the house. I don't know why I feel this way, don't know what I'd do to keep her from getting inside, but I'm suddenly over-whelmed with the knowledge that I need to keep her out here with me.

"Mommy and Daddy were fighting," she finally says, confirming my thoughts. "And Knox and I couldn't sleep."

"You okay, buddy?" I drop to a crouch in front of the two of them and lightly wipe a tear from the boy's cheek. "It's no fun when parents fight, is it?"

He shakes his head.

"What were they fighting about?"

Knox doesn't answer, but I didn't really expect him to. It's Penelope who draws herself up a few inches, like making herself a bit taller will give her the strength she needs to tell me what's going on in the house. I have to fight to tear my eyes away from Knox's face and look up at her.

"They were fighting about you."

My stomach drops. It's what I thought, of course, the thing that makes sense when you consider it. Of course they would fight about me. James hates me, and she's terrified of me and what our friendship could become if she were willing to let down her walls and let me in.

"They were fighting about me?" She nods, and I press the issue. "What were they saying?"

She hesitates, and the low rumble of fear I felt growing in the back of my mind starts to turn into a roar. I need to know what in the world James and Eliza were saying about me. I'd been worried about walking up to their house and knocking on the front door, in case they wanted to hurt me, and I'm beginning to think that my fears were rational.

"They hate you," Penelope says, then adds quickly, "but we don't. We left the house because they scared us."

"I'm sorry they scared you." The pounding in my head has gotten stronger. I glance at the front windows. The two shadows are still there, still talking, but I have no idea how much longer they're going to stand there and talk.

I need to get out of here, but I need something that will guarantee I stay safe.

I think back to my car, to the papers I have in the passenger seat that outline everything I've learned about Knox. All the proof of Eliza and James taking him is right there. I like to keep it with me in case something happens, in case I ever need it. It's like a security blanket.

"They want to kill you," Penelope finally says. I rip my eyes away from the front window of the house and stare at the little girl. She's let go of Knox's hand and is wringing her fingers together like she has to have a way to work out the stress she feels.

"What?"

"They want to kill you so that you can't keep coming around, but Knox and I don't want that. We like you, Bethany." Sweet girl, she lifts her chin, staring at me like she's sure she's making the right decision to put her trust in me.

I think about all of the pictures her mother has made her pose for, all of the times she's chosen Penelope over Knox, even though she was more than willing to kidnap the little boy. Penelope loves her mother, I'm sure of it, but something is wrong.

"Is that why you were running? Were you coming to tell me?"

She shakes her head. "We didn't know you were going to be here. I just had to get Knox out, had to get away from what they were saying."

I'm about to tell her how much I appreciate what she just did for me, that I love her and her brother, and I wouldn't ever do anything to hurt them. I want to leave here, to have more time to think through what I'm going to do and how I can use the information I have on James and Eliza to keep them from hurting me in the future, but before I can even think about how to put those words together into a sentence, the figures in front of the window move away from it.

"We have to go," I say, grabbing Knox by the hand. It's

stupid, foolhardy, but the only thing I can think of to do right now. "We need to move, all of us. Come on."

A chill runs down my spine as he takes a step towards me, willingly following me as I pull him away from the house, but Penelope doesn't move.

"Penelope!" I hiss the little girl's name; she looks at me, then turns and looks over her shoulder at the house. "Penelope, I'm not going to let your parents hurt me, but I can't just stand here with you two. Come on." While I wait for her to respond, I squat down and scoop Knox into my arms.

He doesn't fight it. He snuggles against me, his little arms wrapping around my neck like I'm the only thing in the world that can keep him safe.

We need to move. I don't want to leave the girl behind, so I reach out for her, trying to take her by the hand, but then I hear Eliza scream from inside the house. I need to move now before they come outside, before they see me holding Knox. Even though it kills me to do it, I turn and run back to my car.

Knox doesn't make a sound.

41

ELIZA

I heard myself scream, but it sounded more like it came from someone else's mouth, like the horror playing out in front of me was something I was watching on TV.

I'll probably never know what pushed me to go check on the kids one more time. I wanted to make sure both Penelope and Knox were sound asleep in their beds, that neither of them was going to wake up, that James and I could take care of Bethany in secret.

The last thing I wanted was for either of them to hear what was going on, wake up, come downstairs, and be scarred forever.

But their rooms are empty.

"Where are they?" I scream the words at James, who followed me up the stairs, asking me the entire time what I was doing. "Where are the kids? They were right here!"

It feels good to scream; another one slips from my lips as I hurry to their playroom, throwing open the door, my heart pounding as I hope against hope that they're going to be inside, the two of them breaking the rule about being out of bed after bedtime.

Honestly, I don't care if they're eating brownies and watching cartoons. All that matters to me is that they're both safe, and as long as they're in the house, then I can be sure they're okay.

But they're not here.

"Check in the kitchen!" I have no idea how the two of them could possibly have gotten down the stairs and past us into the kitchen without us noticing, but the conversation James and I were just having was intense.

It's hard to focus on much else when you're trying to work out the details of how to kill someone with your spouse.

James tears down the stairs to check the kitchen. I hurry into the bathroom, turning on the lights and looking in the tub for the kids. It's one thing for one of them to be missing, to think that hiding from us would be an okay idea, but for both of them to be gone... that's strange.

That's concerning.

"She took them," I say, running down the hall into my bedroom. James and I have the biggest one in the house, of course, but this also means there are plenty of places for a little kid to hide if they wanted to try to get away from us. I turn on the lights, dropping to my knees to look under the bed before checking both closets.

Racking my brain to remember all of the hiding spots the two of them use when playing hide-and-seek, I work method-ically through the room, forcing myself to slow down a little bit so I can be sure I don't miss anything.

They're not here.

I have no idea where they are, but I do know they're not in the house.

My knees threaten to give way under me, but I refuse to sink down to the floor, refuse to be a victim in this. I'm going to find my kids.

There's a little voice in the back of my head telling me

that this is what Camilla went through when she finally woke up enough to realize that Knox was gone. She'd reached out to me, panicked and crying, but I only talked to her once before changing my number.

It was cruel, heartless, but when I was holding Knox and trying to take care of him, the last thing I wanted was to talk to his mother. Instead, I watched the news, read in the papers about him going missing. I saw how she tried to pull herself together, kick the drug habit, and did her best to get her life back on track, but it was too little too late.

Whatever progress she made while terrified she'd never get her son back was immediately lost when she started using again to dull the pain she felt after he disappeared. She went to jail and got out, but never reached out to me again.

At least, not that I know of.

I never understood that pain, but now it cuts through me like a hot knife. My entire body hurts, and I just want to curl up into a ball and cry. But that won't bring my kids home.

"Eliza! The front door!" James calls up to me. I force myself to stand, suddenly dizzy. I grab the banister to keep my balance as I hurry down the stairs.

"Did they go outside?"

"It's unlocked!"

From my vantage point as I descend the staircase, I watch as he throws the door open, flicking on the porch light. I'm hopeful, but part of me is convinced that he's going to open the door, and nothing will be there. I'm almost sure of the fact that my kids are gone, that there isn't any way to get them back, that all we can do now is hope that whoever took them will return them.

Bethany.

Her name hits me like a ton of bricks, and I stumble on the last step, grateful to be on the first floor when I find my footing again. I know it's her. There's the sound of running feet outside, and I watch in horror as Penelope runs up the porch steps and into the light.

Tears stream down her cheeks. Her eyes are wide, like she can't believe what she just saw, and she's twisting her night-gown in her hands. I take in all the little details, the pink ribbons at the wrists, the way the lace falls just about her knees, and then I finally drag my eyes back up to my daughter's face.

"He's gone," she gasps. Then James scoops her up, her face pressed against his shoulder. I can't hear what she's saying, and I grab her, pulling her back from his body.

"What? What did you say?" I demand. Penelope cries harder. My fingers sink into her shoulder as I try to get her to answer me. When I see that I'm hurting her, I drop my hand. "Penelope, what did you say?"

"I'm sorry! I'm so sorry we left, but I heard what you were saying about Bethany, and I don't want you to kill her!"

My heart sinks. "You heard that?"

She nods. "We *like* Bethany. I told Knox we needed to leave, that we couldn't be here when you hurt her."

"Honey, where is Knox now?" It's a battle to keep my voice calm when speaking to her, but I'm doing my best. I don't want her to know how I want to scream right now, how just waiting on her to respond to me is making me feel helpless. "Where's your brother? Did he run away?"

Finally, Penelope lifts her head from her father's shoulder and turns to look at me. Her cheeks are splotchy and red, and she wipes snot away from her nose with the back of her hand, but I don't bother to correct her. All that matters is knowing where Knox is.

I need to get him home, need to make sure he's safe.

More than that, I need to get him home so the rest of us are safe. I don't want all of this falling apart because the kids overheard what we were saying. I'm not going to let Bethany be the reason I lose my family.

"He didn't run away," she says, sniffling. "She took him."

"Bethany?" I have to ask, even though I already know. Still, I force myself to say her name, force myself to look at my daughter while I wait for her response.

Penelope nods, then buries her face back in James' shoulder.

He stares at me, unsure of what to do.

It's just like the day we took Knox. I was the person who knew what we had to do, and I was the person who made sure it all happened. It's all falling on my shoulders again. I want James to take control, to fix this—but he can't, or won't, and I know what I have to do.

What *we* have to do.

"Get the car," I tell James. "We're going after our son."

42

BETHANY

Getting Knox in the backseat of my car was the easy part, but now I'm not sure what I need to do or where I need to go. The engine turns over on the first try, and I say a little prayer of thanks as I glance up at the house.

I tear away from Eliza's house just as the front porch light flicks on. I watch in horror in my rearview mirror as Penelope runs up to the porch before being scooped up by James.

We made it out of there, but just in time. I have no doubt in my mind that they're going to do something.

Call the police, maybe? No. Not a chance. If I had Penelope with me, they might. If I had taken the one child they could prove was theirs, then I have no doubt in my mind that the police would be on my tail in no time flat. I'd be really screwed then.

But Knox isn't someone they can prove belongs to them. Because of that, he's not just a child. He's my protection.

"We're going to get some ice cream," I tell him, hoping that will calm him down. He keeps whimpering, not really crying, but moaning and keening like a little puppy. If he spoke more, then I might be able to get him to confirm that he understood what we were doing, but he's never been a big talker.

"I have ice cream at my apartment. Would you like to go get some?" I ask the question before I realize how stupid that is. Of course my apartment is going to be the first place Eliza and James come check when they chase me down. *If they ever found out where I live.* I can't assume that they're not already in their car, already behind me, eating up the road between us.

Nervous, I look in my rearview mirror. There are lights back there, but they're not gaining on me. I exhale hard in relief.

They'll come, but they're not yet.

But then where the hell can we go? I don't want to leave town with him; taking him like this wasn't ever going to be a permanent thing. I just acted in the moment, reacting with horror to what Penelope told me about her parents.

The thought that she and James were talking about how to kill me, of all things, sends a shiver up my spine. It's horrifying, and I squeeze the steering wheel, taking a few deep breaths to try to calm myself down.

Maybe I can go to Cindy's. I think hard, trying to remember if she's working tonight or if she'll be at her place. It isn't a permanent solution—that much I'm sure of—but it should give me some time to think about what to do next.

And her apartment is close enough to mine that I should be able to stay hidden while still keeping an eye out for Eliza.

"Okay, we're going to go see my friend Cindy," I say to Knox, who's still curled up in the backseat. I got the seatbelt on him, but he has his knees pulled up to his chest, his arms wrapped around them like he's trying to make himself as small as possible. "I think you'll like her," I say, fully aware that I'm now rambling. "She's nice, and she always has ice cream."

No response.

I'm speeding, and I know I should slow down, but I press down harder on the gas, urging my car to go as fast as possible so I can get off the road. I need to pull into Cindy's parking lot, park under a dead streetlamp, and wait this out. Or maybe get to her apartment so I can think things through.

There's hardly anyone on the road. Besides the one car behind me that has since pulled off, I've only seen a few other drivers. It's not late enough for people to be in bed, but it is dark and cold out, and I know I'd much rather be curled up in front of the TV right now, but Eliza forced my hand.

This is all on her.

But I think I know how to get her to back off. Eliza has thrown away any chance she had at being my friend, but that doesn't mean I can't walk away from all of this.

Taking my hand off the wheel for just a moment, I grab my phone, swipe it on, and press the speed dial to call her.

She picks up on the first ring. "Where's my son?"

I wince, even though her words can't hurt me. "Eliza, you need to back off," I tell her, looking again in my rearview mirror. "I can prove what you did, that you kidnapped him."

"What?" She hisses the word, and I nod even though she can't see me.

"I have proof." It's right here next to me. "I have everything I need to prove that you took him, that he's not yours— and what do you think the police will do then? You can't kill me. They'll come for you."

"You're insane! You're—"

I don't want to hear what I am. I hang up on her, tossing my phone into the passenger seat.

My mind races. Honestly, I thought that would be enough to make her back off. She wants to kill me, according to Penelope, but if she does that, then the police will come right to her, thanks to the information I have.

I just need to get it to someone who can give it to the police if I go missing.

I really need to make it to Cindy's.

The car coming towards me flicks his high beams at me, and I use one hand to cover my eyes. "Driving like a maniac, that one," I say, but Knox doesn't understand. "Why would someone flick their high beams at another driver like that? It's rude is what it is, and that's how you cause an accident."

Glancing in my rearview mirror, I see another car behind me. They're gaining on me, and I gun it, now going fifteen over the speed limit in an effort to get the hell off the road.

It's only when I pass the abandoned gas station on the right that it hits me why the car coming towards me was flashing his lights at me. But by the time the blue lights fill my car, it's too late for me to slam on my brakes.

43

EIZA

"There! Right there in front of us!" Blue lights light up the night, cutting through the dark, and I lean forward to point at them, my hand braced on the dash as James hurtles us towards the police car. "They pulled her over! We can get Knox back!"

But James doesn't slow down. He zips past the police car and the car it's pulled over, the two of them angled into a church parking lot, the blue lights still whipping through the air.

"What are you doing? He's in that car! Go back there, and we'll get him back!" I grab James' arm, yanking on it like that's going to be enough to get him to turn back around. "Knox is back there! What the hell are you doing?"

"And how do you think this is going to go?" James' voice is dark as he looks over at me. The expression on his face is enough to get me to drop his arm, and I tuck my hands into my lap, squeezing them together as I try to stay calm. "Oh, hello, Officer, yes, this is our son, but we have no proof he's ours. The entire time Bethany will be screaming about how he doesn't belong to us."

I exhale like I was just punched in the stomach. "No, they wouldn't believe her; they'd believe us. We're his parents! And she wants to be my friend. I'll just tell her I want to be friends, that it was all a misunderstanding. I'll get her to see that she can finally have what she wants—"

"She kidnapped him!" He smacks his hand onto the steering wheel and yanks it hard, pulling into a parking lot. I can still easily see the blue lights from here, but there's no way to tell what's going on. "Eliza, you don't think she's willing to tell the truth to the police? Fuck! That's what she's threatened to do since she found out about him!"

Penelope squeaks in the backseat.

"James." My voice is low and calm. "James, you and I both need to calm down. For Penelope."

Twisting around in the seat, he looks at our daughter. "Honey, I'm so sorry. I didn't mean to swear. I'm just worried because we want to get Knox back. I'm sure you understand that, right?"

"Is Bethany going to hurt him?" Her little voice is so small, so scared.

"No, baby," I say, turning to look at her. "Bethany is confused, but we're going to get your brother back. We just have to figure out the best way to do that."

The only problem is that I have no idea how.

"We have to go get him," I say to James. When I turn to look at my husband, though, a shiver of fear runs through me. His jaw is set tight, a frown creasing his forehead. Silently, I will him to look at me, to give me some indication that he thinks we're going to make it through this in one piece, but all I see when I look at him is doubt and concern.

"James." I need to snap him out of this state he's in, to help me decide what we have to do. We need Knox back, we need to get him away from Bethany and the police, and we have to do it without her telling the officer the truth.

"I don't know what to do." James stares at me, and the lost expression on his face makes my stomach drop. "I don't know how we're going to get him back."

"We just have to try." Penelope starts crying in the back-seat, and I know I should turn to her, should offer her some comfort, but the only thing I can think about right now is how terrified Knox must be in Bethany's car. "We have to go back! He's our son!"

For a moment, I think James isn't going to listen to me. I have a sinking sensation that he's going to pull back out onto the road in the direction we were going, that he's going to make me leave my little boy behind, that my life is going to fall apart.

Groaning, he shifts the car back into drive and pulls out onto the road, angling the car not away from Bethany and Knox, like I feared he would, but back in the direction we came, towards my baby, towards the woman who stole him.

"We're going to get your brother back," I say to Penelope. For her part, my daughter is mostly sucking in huge gasps of air and trying to hold it together. I know I shouldn't be angry at her, but if she hadn't left the house, if she hadn't made a run for it...

Shaking my head, I try to clear away the thoughts.

Blue lights get brighter and brighter as we near the parked car. It's so dark out that I'm having trouble making sense of what's going on, and I can't tell where the officer is —but suddenly our beams flash across him. My heart stops.

He's at the driver-side window, his feet shoulder-width apart, his body angled forward a little bit like he's trying to say something to Bethany, trying to get something through to her.

I take in the way he's standing, the strength in his pose, and then I see something else.

He has his gun out and is pointing it right in the driver's window.

44

BETHANY

Knox won't stop crying.

Maybe if he could catch his breath and give me a moment's silence, then I'd be able to figure out what I need to do, but I've already taken too long in getting out of the car or in handing over my information, so that when I turn back to look at the officer to try to explain again what's going on, there's a gun pointed right in my face.

The barrel looks huge.

"Ma'am, I pulled you over for speeding, and I need you to get out of the car. You need to keep your hands where I can see them, refrain from reaching for anything. Get out of the car slowly; let me see your hands as you do. I don't like that you're not showing them to me."

I've been afraid before, when I was younger, when I fell out of a tree or got caught in a riptide at the beach, but what I'm feeling now is nothing compared to that. It's all-encompassing, the type of fear that makes my entire body feel dipped in ice. Even though I'm aware the officer is saying something, I can't make out his words; all I can do is stare in horror at the gun.

"I can prove everything," I say, slowly raising my hands so he can see them. Isn't that what I'm supposed to do, to show that I'm not a threat, that I have no intention of making it so he can't walk away from this encounter in one piece? "He's not my son, but I can tell you what happened."

I don't even realize how much of a mistake I just made until the officer reacts. His face twists in anger, and the blue lights flashing off it make it look even more grotesque and dangerous. I gasp.

"You need to step out of the car! Move slowly; don't do anything stupid. Just get out of the car and keep your hands where I can see them." For just a moment, it sounds like he's underwater; I have to really concentrate to try to understand what he's saying. His voice is hard, and I finally make out the words he's saying, but he doesn't get it.

He doesn't get that I have proof of what Eliza did. "You don't understand! Let me explain, okay? I was speeding, but I have a reason!" I tried to explain it when he pulled me over, tried to make him see that the only reason I have Knox is because his mother lives in Canada and that his aunt stole him.

His eyes are wide, and I realize I can explain all I want, but it won't matter. There's only one thing he heard.

Knox isn't my son.

"Out! Now!"

"I'm coming!" If Knox would just *shut up*, just for one moment, just long enough for me to think, then I'd be able to find my driver's license and my insurance and maybe show this officer the paperwork I have that will prove what Eliza and James did to Knox. I just can't think straight, not with him screaming and carrying on.

I swear he hasn't taken a breath since I got him strapped in the back of the car and tore away from his house. He *knows me*, for God's sake, so I don't know why the hell he's throwing such a fit now.

"Knox, shut up!" I know full well that's not going to do anything to help, but I can't think straight. It's taking all of my self-control to listen to the officer and try to do what he's telling me to, and Knox is making it harder than it should be. "I'm trying to think!"

I'm spun around in my seat, staring at the little boy. His face is shrouded in darkness, but I can still make out the gaping hole of his mouth when he screams. Rage rushes through me, and I want to reach back into the back and *make* him shut up so I can get us out of this.

"Ma'am, you need to exit the car!" The officer is yelling, probably doing his best to make himself heard over Knox screaming the way he is, but there's just one thing I need. I whip back around in my seat to grab it. I'll grab the one thing that will prove it all, prove what I've been doing is the right thing, and then I'll get out of the car.

I know I need to get out and comply with this man. I know I need to listen to him and let him search me and then look in the car to find the information I've collected on Eliza and James himself, but it's *right there*.

"Just give me one second," I say, finally unhooking my seatbelt. My hands are shaking from trying to keep from falling apart, and I reach over to the passenger seat to grab the folder I need. "It's all right here. You just have to look at it, okay?"

He doesn't respond.

He doesn't have to.

45

ELIZA

The sound of gunfire makes every muscle in my body clench. My mouth drops open without me even realizing it, and a sick sound fills the car. It isn't until James slams on the brakes, pulling us over to the side of the road, and reaches over to me to shake me by the shoulder that I realize the sound is coming from me.

"Knox!" Wrenching away from James, I throw the car door open and stumble out of it. There isn't any traffic on the road, but I don't think I would have seen it even if cars were flying at me from both directions. I run to the car, to the officer, to my baby, tears streaming down my cheeks. "Knox!"

The officer was leaning in the window, his hand on his radio, his gun back on his hip, but at the sound of me coming up behind him, he whips around, his eyes hard, his face contorted. "Ma'am, I need you to stay where you are!"

I freeze, skidding to a stop just ten feet from the car. I'm so close I can hear Knox screaming. I crane my neck, looking at the back windows, trying to see my baby.

"My son," I gasp out, "she took my son; he's in that car; his name is Knox. She kidnapped him, and we were trying to get him back, and you pulled her over, and I need him." The words pour out of me in a rush.

Vaguely, I become aware of James at my side. He loops his arm around my waist, and I lean into him, letting him support me.

"You're saying she took your son?"

James speaks up. "Yes, she... she was a friend, and she kidnapped him from the front yard. Our daughter told us what happened, and we got in the car to chase her down and get him back."

"Did you call the police?"

"No, God, no, I just wanted him back!" I take a step closer to the car, then another when the officer doesn't try to stop me. "Please, he's my baby. I just need Knox back."

"I need identification." Walking forward to meet the two of us, he stops us where we are.

I pat my pockets, and I'm horrified that I don't have my purse. "It's at home," I whisper, turning to look at James. "Do you have something? Do you have anything that we can use to prove who we are?"

James nods, moving slowly as he pulls his wallet from his back pocket before extracting his driver's license and handing it over. The officer takes it, then steps back, shining his flash-light on the piece of plastic before speaking into his radio again.

"Is he okay?" I know I should listen to what the officer is saying, but I can't help focusing on Knox. He's screaming, sounding like he's hurt, but I think he's just scared. Bethany wouldn't have hurt him. She didn't have the time. That's the only thing keeping me from losing my mind right now.

If she had hurt him, then I don't know what I would have done. But she's dead.

She's dead.

It's over.

I just want my baby back.

Then it hits me, what she said to me when we called her on the way here, that she has everything she needs to prove that we kidnapped Knox, and a cold chill races through my body. Keeping one eye on the officer, who's still on his radio, I turn to my husband.

"Do you think she really has proof of everything?" My voice is low to keep the officer from overhearing, and James doesn't look at me. I claw at his arm, desperate for him to turn to me, for him to look at me and help me through this. "James, do you think she really does?"

"I don't know." He still hasn't looked away from the officer. "I have no idea, Eliza, but if she does, and he finds it..."

He doesn't finish his thought, but he doesn't have to. I know what will happen, just like he does. If Bethany had proof of us kidnapping Knox, and kept it in the car with her, then they're going to find it.

They're going to come for us.

It won't matter that she's dead and can't bother us any longer, because the two of us will be in jail.

"Please, can we just take him home?" I step away from James, holding my hands up in front of my body so the officer will see I'm not a threat. "Look," I say when he doesn't respond. I pull my phone from my pocket and swipe it on, turning it to show him all the pictures of Knox I have.

Just because I never posted them online doesn't mean I never took them. I have them, proof that the little boy still screaming in the back of the car is ours. They're just not something anyone ever sees.

"Please, he's our boy, and he needs to be out of that car. I know you're going to need statements, you're going to need information, but you have to understand, we can't do this to him. I just want to get him home, want to make sure he's safe. I need to hold him and let him know that he's okay."

Tears spring to my eyes, and my voice breaks. For just a moment, I think the officer is going to refuse me, but he nods.

"Backup is on the way," he tells the two of us, looking at James and then locking his eyes on his face. He hands James his wallet, and I can feel the relief pouring off my husband. "This is a crime scene now, and we're going to have to get techs out here. It's going to be a long night, but there's no reason why your family has to stand here on the side of the road."

He shines his light at our car, and I see Penelope's little face staring through the window.

"I just want to get the kids home," I say. "We'll answer whatever questions you have when you're ready to talk to us."

"You can take them," the officer says, "but wait here."

Before we can respond, he walks over to Bethany's car. I'm holding my breath, a fact I only realize when he has the back-seat open and leans in to unbuckle Knox. A moment later, the little boy runs over to the two of us, slamming into my legs.

I pick him up, and he buries his face in my neck.

"Oh, Knox," I tell him, rubbing his back. "You're okay, you're okay. I promise you, things are going to be okay."

"Thank you, Officer," James says, "thank you for saving our boy." His voice breaks.

The sound of sirens getting closer makes the hair on the back of my neck stand up. I have to remind myself that they're not here for us. They're here for Bethany, and she can never hurt us again.

Only, she can.

The officer walks over with James to our car. He's getting the tag number, and I watch as he writes it down. Then I hurry over to Bethany's car, knowing I need to look through the window even though the last thing I want to see is her body.

"Don't look, baby," I tell Knox as I squeeze him tighter.

It's dark in the car, and I have to force myself to look away from Bethany. She's slumped over across the middle console like she was reaching for something, and it only takes me a moment to see what it was.

Sure, the manila folder is splattered with blood.

Sure, it will probably take the police a little while to get to the contents and find out she was telling the truth.

But once they do, they'll know it all.

I want to open the passenger door and grab the folder. I want to take it and burn it, ruin Bethany's chances of ever ruining my life. But then sirens fill the air, making me freeze. James is calling me, and I have to turn away from the car, pretend I wasn't looking.

Pretend I didn't just see the one thing that will bring it all crashing down around our heads.

46

ELIZA

"I saw it," I say to James, turning my head just a little to look at him. Knox is asleep on my chest, his little body hot with fear and stress. While I know I should get him upstairs and into his bed so that he can sleep better than he will sprawled across me right now, there's no way I'm moving.

I don't want to put him down, and I certainly don't want him to wake up and think that his dad and I abandoned him. He and Penelope were both a hot mess when we got them home, but she passed out shortly after James carried her into the house. Now she's in bed where she belongs.

Right now, though, I just don't think I can put Knox down. I need to feel his little body on mine, need to feel his hot breath on my cheek. We were so close to losing him, to *losing everything*, and while I'd like to think that threat is over, it's not.

And James and I both know it.

"Saw what?" James is exhausted. I can see it in the lines on his face, and I know he's close to falling asleep here on the sofa next to me. How he can sleep after this is beyond me, but I have enough adrenaline for both of us.

"The folder she told us she had. It wasn't a bluff, James. I thought it might be, but it was right there in the passenger seat. She was going to give it to the police if..." I can't finish the thought.

Looking in the car was one of the dumbest things I've ever done, but I had to. I had to know that she was really gone, and I had to know if the folder was really there. She was gone, and it was there, and now I'm going to have to live with that mental image burned into my brain for the rest of my life.

"Did you open it? We don't know if it really had what she claimed it did, or if she was just trying to make us think that she could hurt us. I know you think it was real, Eliza, but we don't know that for sure, right? We have no way of really knowing that."

I think about Bethany, about how careful she was when finding me and making me spend time with her. I think about how she stalked me, how she inserted herself into my life, how she made sure she had all the information she needed to ensure we would spend time with her, and I shake my head.

"I believe it," I tell him, still keeping my voice low. Knox could probably sleep through an earthquake right now, but I'm not willing to risk that and accidentally wake him up, at least not until James and I know what we're going to do.

"Okay, so what does that mean for us?" His eyes are closed, like he just can't keep them open any longer. I wish he would look at me while the two of us are talking, but he's falling asleep right here.

"It means that they're going to find it. The car is a crime scene, James; you heard the officer. You think that they're not going to look in that folder when they get it all cleaned up?

Hell, they could be looking in it now." Glancing towards the front windows, I'm half expecting to see blue lights in our driveway.

"And then what?" His eyes are finally open. "You think they'll come here on the word of someone they just killed? On the word of someone who kidnapped our son? Don't forget, Eliza, in the eyes of the law, she's the one who did something wrong, not us."

"Only because they don't know that we did it, too." The irony of Bethany kidnapping Knox from us when we did the same to my sister isn't lost on me; I just don't want to admit it and think about how it makes me feel. "Believe me, I really don't think the police are going to take it easy on us once they figure out that we did the exact same thing to him a year and a half ago."

"I just don't think they'll take the word of a criminal."

"Jesus, James, really? You don't think they're going to look into every little aspect of this? You don't think someone isn't *right now* flipping open that folder and looking up Camilla? Because I do. I'm terrified that they're going to look into this, they're going to realize that Bethany was crazy but she wasn't lying, and they're going to come take him away."

"This is a conversation for tomorrow." James stands up, turning to stare at me. "I love you, Eliza, but I need to sleep on this. I need to clear my head before I can think about what the hell we're going to do."

"James." I have to shift Knox to reach out for James, to grab his hand, and my son stirs, grunting a little, but I don't care. I need my husband to listen to me, to really pay attention to what I'm saying, and he can't seem to do that. "We don't have the luxury of waiting to deal with this later. The police aren't going to wait."

"The police are overworked and underpaid. They're going to get the car into some building somewhere so that techs can work on it in the morning. Right now, their main concern is dealing with the body. Come on, I know you think it's all going to come crashing down around your head, but we need sleep. I can't come up with anything to do without some sleep, and you look like you're about to fall apart."

I feel like I am, but I don't want to admit that to him. When he moves to take Knox from me, I don't resist, just help him lift our son up so he can carry him to his bed.

The entire time I watch him go, though, I know he's wrong.

James thinks that we have time, but time is a luxury that is only afforded to people who haven't done something like kidnap their nephew. If he doesn't want to worry about what will happen to our family, that's fine, but I'm not going to rest.

There's only a few hours until everything falls to pieces, and I'm not going to spend them with the covers pulled over my head, pretending that everything is going to be fine when I'm sure it won't.

That's the one thing I've learned—if you want something, you have to take it.

If you need something to happen—you have to be the one willing to go out on a limb to make it happen.

James isn't willing to do that, but I am.

I'm going to save this family.

47

JAMES

I'm exhausted.

After last night and the fitful sleep I got after putting Knox to bed, all I wanted to do was stay home with Eliza and the kids, but that simply wasn't possible. I knew I needed to get to work, put on a brave face, pretend like everything was okay. She was frantic thinking that something terrible was going to happen last night, but that's the difference between the two of us.

I know that terrible things take time to happen. I see it all the time with my patients. So while Eliza thought for sure the police were going to show up at our door last night, I knew they had to get all of their ducks in a row.

I have no idea what time she came to bed since I never heard her, but this morning she was up, dressed, and ready to start the day when I made it downstairs for breakfast.

The kids looked exhausted, but nobody mentioned what happened last night. She kissed me goodbye, told me to have a great day, then went back inside to make sure the kids were eating their breakfast.

Nothing new, nothing out of the ordinary.

Now, on the way home, there's something in the pit of my stomach, a feeling that I made a mistake going to work, that I should have called in sick, done whatever I could to be with my wife and kids.

It doesn't help that the news of the police shooting someone in their car last night was all anyone seemed to be able to talk about at work, and it certainly doesn't help that Eliza hasn't answered my calls or texts all day long. I've texted her a few times and called her twice, and both times I've gone unanswered.

That's abnormal for my wife. She's normally attached to her phone, normally has it pressed up against her ear or open on her palm so she can deal with whatever her readers need to know, so the fact that she hasn't answered me is not only weird, it's concerning.

The pit in my stomach only gets worse when I turn onto our street and see the cop cars lining the road. They're pulled off almost into the ditch, parked all along the grass my neighbor has tried to grow for years, all the way up to our driveway, which is full of cars.

I slam on the brakes, unsure of what I need to do.

My phone is in my cupholder, and I fumble it out, thumb it on, then call my wife one more time.

Where the hell is she?

Again, just like I suspected, she doesn't pick up the phone. My heart slams in my chest. "Eliza, it's James. I don't know where the hell you are or why you aren't picking up, but I just got home from work, and there are a ton of police here. I'm going to go to the house, but I need to know if you're okay. If the kids are okay." I pause, unsure of what else to say or how I can get through to my wife that I'm not only worried about her, but that she needs to call me back as soon as possible. "Call me. You'd better be at home."

Even as I tap the red circle to hang up, though, I know something is terribly wrong.

Eliza was terrified the police were going to find Bethany's proof of us taking Knox.

She was upset with me last night that I didn't seem to be as worried as she was. I thought we had more time; I thought they would take longer to go through Bethany's car, to learn what really happened with Knox. There wasn't any way I thought they'd get around to it that quickly, that they'd be on our doorstep this evening.

Before I know what I'm doing, I put the car back in drive and start to work my way down the street, keeping my eyes straight ahead, doing everything that I can to avoid making eye contact with one of the few officers milling around.

Then it hits me.

I'm in the same car we were driving last night, the same one the officer stood behind to take down the tag number.

I press down harder on the gas. It's a risk, but one I have to be willing to take. Eliza must have already been caught, but the thought of driving up and parking and turning myself over to an officer makes me sick.

That explains why she isn't answering her phone. That explains everything, why I can't get in touch with her, why there are so many police here, why I've felt all day like I was going to be sick.

She was right. We should have done something last night or this morning. We should have run, done whatever it took to save ourselves and our kids.

I wish I'd listened to her.

I press down harder on the gas. Our house is now on my right, and all I need to do is make it to the cul-de-sac, turn around, and head back out of the neighborhood so I can figure out what I'm going to do. If they've already picked Eliza up, if the police already have her, then I'm not sure what she's told them.

Would she have blamed this entire thing on me? The thought is terrifying, but it's all I can think about as I inch my car forward, praying that the officers won't turn around and look at me.

I'm fine, until they do.

An officer turns, obviously having heard my car, and almost does a double take when he sees me. He moves quickly, stepping right in front of my car, his hand out, his other hand resting easily on his gun.

Shit.

Another officer turns and looks, and a moment later he's at my window, an angry look on his face, his hand resting on his gun, already gesturing for me to roll down my window.

I freeze, then do what he wants.

"Dr. Sullivan?"

I don't want to answer him, don't want to nod, but I do anyway, unable to stop myself from moving, from doing what he wants me to do.

"James Sullivan, I need you to get out of the car."

I put the car in park, doing everything slowly, making sure my hands are in plain view. The image of what happened to Bethany last night is seared into my memory, and I finally open the door, stepping out, the engine still running.

"Dr. Sullivan, where is your wife?"

"What?" I heard what he said, but I can't seem to wrap my mind around the question. "What do you mean where's Eliza? She's with you."

A radio squawks, but neither of the officers moves to answer it. Instead, the one closest to me shakes his head. "Dr. Sullivan, we've been unable to locate your wife or the children. Have you been in contact with her?"

I'm lost. It feels like the world is crashing down around me, and I know I need to answer him, but I can't seem to focus on what he's saying. "She's gone?"

This entire time I thought for sure the police had her. I thought Eliza was in police custody, that they had her in for questioning, but I must have been wrong.

I was wrong.

"She's gone, and we need to talk to you about the child living with you, Knox. Do you know where he is?"

"Knox?" I can't seem to form any sentences. All I can do is parrot the officer's words back to him, unsure of what I'm really saying.

"We have enough to take him in." The other officer finally speaks. When I look at him, his gaze cuts into me. "Let's take him to an interview room."

"An interview room? Where is my wife? Where are Penelope and Knox?" Even as I ask the questions, though, I know where they are.

"Dr. Sullivan, I need you to come with me." A beefy hand lands on my shoulder, and I flinch away from it, but the officer doesn't drop it.

"The kids are gone? And my wife? They're really gone?"

It all makes sense. All of it. The fact that Eliza never got in touch with me today. How upset she was with me last night for not being willing to do something about Knox right away.

"She left me," I say, turning to the officer. It's not that I expect sympathy from him, but something would be better than the look on his face. "She took them and left me."

"We have a lot to talk about," he says, pulling me away from my car.

I'm aware that the neighbors are watching. That my car is still running.

But those things don't matter. The only thing I can really think about is Eliza.

And the fact that she left me here to try to clean up her mess on my own.

48

ELIZA

Ten Hours Earlier

"It's time to go," I announce at the breakfast table. Knox and Penelope both look at me in surprise. He still has a smear of maple syrup on his fat little cheeks, and while Penelope has finished, she keeps eyeballing the stack of pancakes.

We could be here all morning if I'm not careful, but I'm not going to let that happen. We need to move because I have a very good feeling that the police are doing the same thing.

Justice doesn't sleep, or some crap like that, and that means I can't either.

And I didn't.

I was up all night packing bags, making sure we'd be ready when it was time to get in the car and put this all behind us. No, I don't want to leave our house, the place where we've made so many memories, but I'll do it if it means keeping my family together. There's no way I'm going to sit here and wait for the police to knock on our door when I know I could get a head start and keep my kids.

They're the only thing in this world that really matters. Bethany should have known that trying to take them from me was going to end badly, but she still did it, and that's why she's dead and I'm not.

Clapping my hands, I push back from the table. "Go wash up, and then I have a surprise for everyone!"

"A surprise?" Penelope looks suspicious and glances at Knox before looking back at me. "What kind of surprise?"

"A good one," I promise. "Last night was so hard, and we've been stuck in this house for so long without a vacation that I thought we'd go to the beach."

Knox's eyes light up, but like always, it's Penelope who speaks for the two of them. "What beach? And why? You told me that we couldn't take a vacation for a while, that Knox needed to be inside because of his skin, that the sun was too much for him."

"Things change. And this is a new beach," I tell her. "One a long way away, so we're going to have to get driving soon." I resist checking my watch, which is something I can't seem to stop doing. "Now get, you two, clean up, then meet me back down here. I packed your bags while you were sleeping."

"Beach!" Penelope raises her little fist above her head and starts to chant as she and Knox push away from the breakfast table. "Beach, beach, beach, beach!"

He doesn't chant with her, but he follows right on her feet, a dutiful little brother. I sigh, bracing my hands on the table for a moment.

It's going to feel weird to walk away from the kitchen table with dishes still on it, but I don't need to clean it up. The piles of dirty laundry, the leftovers that will rot in the refrigerator, none of it matters.

We'll swing by the bank on the way out of town, get as

much cash as we can, then head straight south. Mexico has an extradition treaty with the United States, but we should be able to cross the border really easily thanks to Penelope's birth certificate and the fake one I made for Knox last night. I have my passport tucked in my purse, and soon we'll be able to put this all behind us. I'm counting on it, then counting on being able to work our way south, make a new home somewhere where nobody can ever find us.

It's a good thing I took all those Spanish classes in college.

The more borders I can put between us and the police, the better. The faster we move, the faster we get on the road, the better.

I'll cut my hair, cut Penelope's, maybe turn myself into a redhead. There are a lot of things we need to do to save ourselves, and we need to get moving.

In just a moment my kids are back, and I usher them to the already-packed car, grabbing my purse and my coffee on the way. At the garage door I pause, then put my phone down on the kitchen counter. The last thing I want is for the police to be able to track me using it.

It killed me not answering James all day, but he made his choice last night when he told me that we had time to wait, that things would shake out just fine.

I'm running on adrenaline and caffeine, a dangerous combination, but one I'm hoping will keep me awake long enough to get out of here, to get far enough away from Tennessee that by the time the police know what's going on, it will be too late for them to find us.

"What about Daddy?" Penelope shrugs on her seatbelt and lets me buckle her in before I make sure Knox is nice and safe next to her. The two of them barely have any room to move, I have the backseat so loaded down with snacks and their favorite toys and books to keep them occupied while I drive.

"Daddy will meet up with us later," I tell her, the lie flowing smoothly off my tongue before I get in the front seat, crank the engine, and back out of the driveway.

What I don't tell her is the truth.

James thought everything was going to be fine. He didn't think we needed to worry.

He never looked in my car this morning before heading to work, never knew that I'd spent so many hours last night packing and planning. He promised me everything would be fine before he kissed me and left for work, and I'd made sure to agree with him.

Because I do.

Everything is going to be fine, but only because I'm willing to do whatever I have to to make sure it will be.

I'm sorry he won't come with us, but the kids and I will be fine without him.

I'll make sure of it.

THANK YOU FOR READING

Did you enjoy reading *The Stolen Child*? Please consider leaving a review on Amazon. Your review will help other readers to discover the novel.

ABOUT THE AUTHOR

Emily Shiner always dreamed of becoming an author but first served her time as a banker and a teacher. After a lifetime of devouring stacks of thrillers, she decided to try her hand at writing them herself. Now she gets to live out her dream of writing novels and sharing her stories with people around the world. She lives in the Appalachian Mountains and loves hiking with her husband, daughter, and their two dogs.